Freeing the Feline

An *Awakening Pride* Story

Freeing the Feline

By Lacey Thorn

Resplendence Publishing
www.resplendencepublishing.com

Published by Resplendence Publishing, LLC
1093 A1A Beach Blvd, #146
St. Augustine, FL 32080

Freeing the Feline

Edited by Delaney Sullivan and Kimberly Huther
Cover Art by Les Byerley

Print format ISBN: 978-1-60735-824-4

Print Release: October 2015

To all the wonderful fans of the Awakening Pride series! Thank you for the outpouring of love! This series would not be possible without your support!

Special thanks to Tia Thomas Blakey and Christy Zito Hebert for all the love and for helping brainstorm titles with me!

To Les, who makes the best covers I've ever seen! Thanks for sharing your brilliance with the rest of us!

And to all the staff at Resplendence Publishing, thank you for all your love and support! You guys are amazing! I'm so lucky to work with you!

Chapter One

Clara was going stir crazy. Her skin itched with the need to shift and go for a run. Hell, just to be out in the fresh air. A week of being locked up in this room with only Logan as a visitor was starting to take a toll on her. She'd been away too long, with no contact with her Uncle Thomas or Lydia. She should have thought to call and check in weeks ago. They must be worried to death over her extended absence. She had to find a way to contact them—a secure way.

Logan had done his best to make her think she was locked up for her safety as well as theirs. Honestly, she couldn't blame them. She'd do the same in their place. She was the outsider, the unknown. Plus, she hadn't gained any brownie points by admitting she'd been basically stalking Amia and had followed her and Reno to Colorado. Then she'd topped it all off by yelling things at the alpha's mate that no woman wanted to hear, much less a very pregnant one.

She tilted her head to look at the ceiling, closed her eyes and heaved a weary sigh. Yeah, she'd lock herself up if she were in their shoes. Her emotions were all over the place, and she'd lost her temper downstairs. She felt overwhelmed and inadequate to deal with anything. It didn't help that everything was so damn confusing. How was she supposed to deal with the fact she knew more than Tah when he was the leader they'd been waiting for? She didn't feel prepared or knowledgeable enough to make decisions that could affect the future of the entire pride. They needed someone far better suited to teach them than she was—someone older and wiser.

She paced to the door and back to the window, the one that was sealed so well she couldn't break out. Of course, Logan had shown her the alarm linked to it just in case she decided to try her hand at it anyway. He'd grinned, all proud of himself, as he'd pointed it out. She was here until they decided otherwise. Yet, that wasn't the problem. No, the problem was she didn't want to leave.

It wasn't even because she'd found Tah. Seeing him stepping toward her for the first time had sent her immediately to her knees. She'd tried to cover it up, to play it off. But God! She'd been told of him since she was born. Part of her had begun to believe he was nothing more than myth and legend. Then there he was, bigger than life, radiating some serious alpha pheromones that had her eager to submit to whatever he wanted her to do. It was bizarre. Especially since he wasn't that much older than she was.

She wondered what her uncle would think of the alpha. Tah wasn't just young; he was untrained, inexperienced and still learning about himself and what it meant to have a pride. This group of his seemed to know so little. Still, he'd already assembled people he trusted— a mixture of human and shifter. And from what she'd overheard, he even had a friendship with the wolf pack, through their alphas no less. That was something even Uncle Thomas had never managed.

There was so much she could teach Tah and the shifters with him. So many things she could educate them about—if she were a little more confident. She'd honestly feel better if she could contact her uncle and have him be the one to come and help them. Uncle Thomas was one of the wisest shifters she knew. He would know where to start and how to go about all of it. Clara was too uncertain, and the current battle she was fighting—the unrelenting urge to mate—left her weak and exposed at a time when she could ill afford it. As much as her focus should be on the alpha she'd spent her entire life waiting for, it was another that claimed her attention and had her desiring to stay, to belong.

Logan Dobson. A human, though no less alpha in his demeanor than the two shifters he called brothers. At first, she'd been confused, until she realized the term brothers didn't refer to a sharing of blood, but of a bond formed in life that made them claim each other as family, as brothers. She could understand that. Shifters didn't always share blood, but that was irrelevant. They were a family none-the-less.

A brief tap sounded at the door before it was shoved open, revealing the man who tormented her by awakening feelings she wasn't prepared to deal with.

"I brought you some lunch," he said as he hit the door with his hip to shut it once more.

She followed him with her gaze as he moved to her bed and sat, putting down the tray and grabbing one of the pillows to place on his lap.

"Join me?"

Did he think she wouldn't know his cock was long and thick, that she couldn't smell the lust and desire on him? Did he know his scent coated the pillow when he left, that she hugged it to her and longed for him to be in the bed with her every night? He was killing her.

"Clara?"

"I'm not hungry."

He laughed and the deep timbre of his husky chuckle washed over her, setting her nipples on fire and leaving her pussy slick with need. She'd known from the first moment she saw him that he was her mate, the man destined to fill her every need. The one person who could make her whole. It was something she'd spent her whole life anticipating. But why here? Why now? Why him, the man keeping her prisoner?

"You have to eat," he crooned, and she shivered.

He grabbed a slice of apple from the tray and brought it to his lips. She heard the crunch as his teeth bit off a piece, saw the damp spray of juice, and she licked her lips in hunger. For him and only him.

"I said I'm not hungry." She turned her back to him and looked out the window. It didn't help. It never helped. She still felt him with every inch of her being. She knew when he was close. It was the way it was with mates. And if she bit him, if she claimed him…

Then she would always know where he was, if he was upset or in danger, and he'd know the same about her. It was a risk she couldn't take, and it was tearing her up.

"All you have to do is talk to me," Logan said as he rose to stand beside her bed. "No more room. You could go anywhere. We just need you to talk, tell us what you know."

"I've told you."

"You've told us only enough to make us aware of how much we don't know. I get that you're angry, but it won't help you to continue alienating yourself from everyone here by throwing out barbs meant to upset people. Every conversation doesn't need to be a battle. We're not your enemy."

"Well, I'm sure you can understand my confusion." She turned and waved her hands around her. "Most friends don't keep you locked up."

She could tell Logan was gritting his teeth by the set of his jaw. She was pissing him off again. She seemed to do that so well.

"I didn't say we were your friends. Maybe if you quit lying to us there would be a chance for that."

"I haven't lied to you."

Logan snorted. "A lie of omission is still a lie."

"I'd say that's subjective."

He shook his head. "It doesn't have to be this difficult. You've been here a week, and we're no closer to answers than we were before you got here. We've only come up with more questions."

"I don't have all the answers you want."

"You have some of them. We know you do. How much longer do you want to play things out this way, because I'm getting damn tired of it."

"Are you threatening me?" She couldn't hold back the rumble of challenge that sounded in her chest, or the way her canines flashed as she snarled at him.

And he grinned. The prick didn't even have the wisdom to be scared of her.

"I hang out with Tah and Reno. You'll have to do better than a flash of teeth and a growl if you want to scare me. And for the record, I don't intimidate easily."

"I could tear you apart with my bare hands." She wouldn't, but he couldn't really know that.

"You could try." He spread his hands wide as if to say, here I am, come and get me. "It's a risk I'm willing to take."

She turned her back to him again. "Go away."

"Not this time."

She heard the grunt of anger in his voice and had just enough time to turn around before he was in front of her, pinning her to the wall. His scent wrapped around her, stroking her like invisible fingers and making her a weak mass of female flesh.

"Don't equate human with being stupid or weak," he gritted out between his teeth.

"I've never thought of you as weak or stupid," she panted.

Her heart galloped as his forearms brushed against her shoulders. He had her caged in, effectively trapped, with no avenue of escape, and they both knew it. Not without her risking hurting him, and she wasn't prepared to do that.

"But you think of me," he whispered, dropping his head so his breath tickled her ear as he spoke. "I hear you call my name at night. I've walked in and seen you thrashing in that big bed, moaning my name. Do you know how hard it is to walk away? Knowing you want me as much as I want you?"

"It's all those dreams of killing you I have. No Stockholm Syndrome here."

He laughed. "We may have been getting rough in your dreams, but the only thing killing either of us was probably the pleasure we're going to unleash when we finally give in."

"I don't know what you're talking about." Oh, but she did, and she wanted. God, how she wanted.

"Do you think I can't pick up on the signals you're throwing out just because I don't have your super senses?" he challenged.

"What signals?" She bit her lip, realizing she'd played right into his hands by the way he leaned even closer, touching her with his body.

"That I can't see the way your pulse picks up every time I enter this room." He dropped his head and ran his tongue over the fluttering point on her neck. The backs of his fingers skimmed across her taut nipples. "That I can't see the way your breasts swell and grow tight. You want my mouth there as much as I want to see and taste you there."

"I…" She moaned, leaning her head back and closing her eyes as he slid his hand over the crotch of her pants and cupped her.

"Do you think I don't know how hot and wet you get for me? Baby, I don't need to be a kitty to pick up on the fact you want me as much as I want you. All I have to be is attentive." He brushed his lips up her neck, along the edge of her jaw, and up to her earlobe. "And I promise, I can be very attentive." He nipped her lobe with his teeth and it took all she had to lock her knees and keep herself upright.

"I can't." She finally forced the words past the lust-filled fog that consumed her.

He was her mate. Neither of them should have to deny what was happening. But there was too much else going on, and Clara was never selfish.

Logan seemed to gather himself and slowly pushed away from her. His stare met hers and she almost lost herself again in the rich chocolate of his gaze. She could drown there, with him, in him.

He stepped back once, twice, dropping his head and shaking it back and forth before looking up at her.

"I know. That's why I'm doing my best to keep my hands off. I don't know why you're denying what's going on between us, but I'll respect it."

"You don't understand—"

"So tell me," he interrupted. "I'm all ears. Talk to me."

"It's not that easy," she reasoned.

"I don't want easy," Logan fired back. "I want you."

"There's more than just the two of us involved here."

"Not at the moment."

"I don't think everyone else is going to back off with what they want just because we ask them to. Not even with a pretty please."

"Then help me out here. Talk to me about what you know. Give me enough to sate them." He locked his gaze on hers. "Then I'll see if I can work on sating us."

Clara shivered. What could she tell them, tell Tah that wouldn't influence their choices? God, this was so fucked up. Tah was the leader they'd all been waiting for, and he'd only just realized who he was. She knew more than he did, yet he was the one who was supposed to guide them all. It just made no fucking sense. She wasn't talking because she honestly had no fucking clue what to say.

"If I could make a call," she urged. "My uncle might be able to come or at least be willing to talk to one of you. He's the one who can help, not me." She shook her head urgently. "I don't know how."

"We can't trust you to make a call out right now. There's a lot at stake, and we can't risk it. You've got to show us we can trust you, Clara. And stalking Amia and Reno isn't the right way."

"I wasn't stalking her or them," Clara argued. She'd been watching over the other woman. She sighed as Logan lifted a brow. She had to admit the fact she'd followed the other couple here looked bad. "How am I going to convince anyone while I'm locked up in here?"

"Maybe if you tried to be a little friendlier with the rest of them..."

She snorted. "I've not exactly been friendly with you, and it hasn't stopped you."

"We both know why I'm not going away," he reminded her, then chuckled again as her cheeks heated.

"Yeah, well, that can't happen, either."

"Scared?"

"Of you? Never!"

He grinned at her. "Then it will happen, baby. The sooner you say yes, the sooner we both release some of the tension building up in us."

She groaned and moved across the room, putting the bed between them. Bad idea. Now all she could do was picture them rolling around on that bed...relieving tension.

"Fuck!" she exclaimed.

"If that's your way of saying yes, count me in."

She couldn't help it. She laughed. "You're crazy."

"I've been told that several times." He sat on the opposite side of the bed and nudged the tray toward her. "I've also been told I'm a good listener."

She sat gingerly on the other side and reached for a slice of apple. "I don't want to hurt you, any of you."

"There's a war coming, Clara. We're not so ill-informed that we don't realize that. Hell, most of us have been soldiers, Marines. We know we can't stop what's coming, but we can prepare for it. We just need to know as much as we can about who we're fighting, something more than we can learn from old journals."

"Hunters in general? Or the Blanes, specifically?"

"Both."

She mulled it over in her head. She should be able to discuss that. She could tell them about her personal experiences, what she'd witnessed, what she'd heard from others. But, what if she let something slip? Damn, she wanted her Uncle Thomas. Only he would understand the precarious position she was in. She'd finally come face-to-face with Amia again, and it had blown all to hell. Amia was angry with her. Clara knew it. How did she explain that she'd done all she could, all she was allowed and still avoid other questions—questions that could lead to answers Amia probably wasn't ready to hear?

"Clara, you can tell me anything. I promise."

She wanted to believe him. She wanted nothing more than to lay herself bare and share her confusion with someone else. Maybe he would know what to say, what to share? But to trust him would mean claiming him as her mate. She couldn't do that. Not yet. Not with everything that lay between them. The one thing she did know for sure was that a confrontation between Amia and Lydia was probably inevitable at this point. And that had Clara terrified.

She still remembered when she turned sixteen and decided to go looking for Amia on her own. She'd almost died, should have died. But Amia had saved her. Clara had called Lydia as soon as they were far enough away from the Blane camp and told Lydia she had Amia. Lydia had blown a fucking gasket and ordered Clara to get the hell away. She'd still been young and naive then, so she'd done as

Lydia had ordered—left Amia alone and helpless against the Blanes. And Clara had lived with the guilt everyday.

Clara had spoken to her Uncle Thomas about Amia as soon as she'd gotten back. He'd been interested enough to have Clara check on Amia again. She'd believed Lydia was right about how blood would tell when Amia was back with the Blanes. She'd stayed and waited, watching and hating Amia for not being the girl Clara had dreamed of, the one she'd thought of as a sister. She was glad she'd stayed. That was when she'd found out what the Blanes were doing to Amia.

Clara had wanted to bring Amia back with her then, but Uncle Thomas had been the one to say no. He was afraid of what it would do to Lydia to have Amia there with them. The other woman was starting to show moments of rage and deep hatred for the Blanes. Her uncle had been afraid of what Lydia might do to Amia. Clara knew he'd sent others to try to watch over and protect Amia, but after the first few were found and killed, volunteers ceased, and Amia seemed to draw into herself, even shunning the humans who'd tried to befriend her.

"Clara?" Logan's voice broke into her thoughts and brought her back to the present.

"I need to make that call," she told him, hating the begging tone of her voice.

He shook his head. "I can't make any promises, but if you start talking—about the Blanes and the hunters—it would be a first step."

"And will this be like the last time I was brought into a room to be questioned?"

"It will probably only be me, Tah and Reno. Maybe the Professor."

"So only four against one this time."

"I won't let that happen again," Logan said. "I promise I'll look out for you."

"I'm not yours to protect."

"You could be."

"I can't do this with you right now, Logan. There's so much more involved here than you and I and scratching an itch."

He grunted. "Fool yourself if you need to, but don't try it with me. We both know what's between us is much more than scratching an itch. The way I'm feeling, I'd say it's pretty clear I'm your mate."

Her eyes widened in shock as she gaped at him. "What?"

"You think I can't figure it out? I was there when Tah and Abby first got together. I've seen Reno and Amia together. We may be learning as we go, but we're fast learners. This physical pull I have toward you… It's not normal, baby. The way my cock is like an iron poker in my pants is not normal. No amount of jacking off gives me any relief. It wants one thing and one thing only. You, anyway you'll let me have you. I feel like a fucking caveman when I'm around you. Hell, just the mention of your name gets me revved. You're mine. I want to beat my chest and drag you to my bed. Fuck until neither of us can move. Maybe if I were more than just a man, I'd press harder to get what we both want." He pushed to his feet and held his arms wide again. "But I'm only human, Clara. I want you. I won't lie or hide the fact, from you or anyone. But I want more than a warm body in my bed. I want a partner, a mate. I want the warmth, but I want the affection and yeah, the love that appears to comes with it. I want it all. So I'll hold back and wait until you want it just as badly."

He turned and headed to the door, opening it slowly before turning to glance her way once more.

"Logan…" She didn't know what else to say other than his name.

"I'll wait. I know you'll be more than worth it."

With that he left, shutting the door behind him. She wanted to scream his name, to beg him to come back to her. She wanted to take, to claim, and to hell with everything and everyone else. But she couldn't. Her uncle would expect more from her. Pride before self. Those were the words he'd told her all her life. She was really having trouble sticking to them right now.

"Uncle Thomas," she whispered. "Please. I need you." She hung her head and let the tears flow. "I need you."

Chapter Two

"So she's agreed to talk," Tah said, leaning back against the desk in the office. "Thanks for checking in with her, Logan. I've been distracted with everything going on with Abby and trying to find Finn. I should have made a point of getting up there to talk to her."

"She said she'll tell you what she knows about hunters and the Blanes in particular," Logan said. He wasn't going to admit he hadn't minded being the only one checking on her over the last week. He'd been hoping to persuade her to give in to what he knew they were both feeling, but Clara was holding back. He was still antsy after their latest encounter. He'd pushed things this time. His cock was swollen to the point it felt as if it was going to burst out of his jeans. As it was, he'd un-tucked his shirt to try and hide the blatant bulge. "This is a step in the right direction."

"I still don't want her around Abby. I won't have my mate upset any more right now if I can help it. She's been having nightmares about Harlan ripping our son out of her womb."

"Jesus," Reno muttered. "Is that why she's looking so exhausted?"

"Who the fuck knows?" Tah rumbled angrily. "She barely eats and has trouble keeping down what she does. She tosses and turns all night long. Her back aches. Her sides ache. Her feet ache. She's one giant fucking ache, and I'm helpless to do anything about it. To know my seed is doing this to her, that I did this to her. Some days, I wish she hadn't been ovulating, that she wasn't pregnant."

"Don't let Abs hear you say that," Logan warned.

Tah was showing the wear and tear of all they'd been through, as well.

"You're looking a little rough yourself," he continued.

"If I can't help her, I can at least be tired and miserable with her," Tah said.

"I take it Diane and the Professor aren't having any luck finding a way to help," Reno said.

"Diane thinks the baby is growing more in line with the gestational period of a lion. Abby's almost twelve weeks along now. If Diane's theory is correct, she'll give birth in another three to four weeks," Tah said.

"Damn!" Logan exclaimed. "That quick?"

"That's the issue. The baby is growing too rapidly. Abby's body isn't adjusting as quickly. This pregnancy is tearing her apart. I can't lose her." Tah's eyes were bleak when he met Logan's gaze.

"We're not going to let that happen," Reno promised, but the words were on the tip of Logan's tongue, as well.

"I could ask Clara. She might know something," Logan offered again.

"Abby won't trust anything Clara says right now. Not after the confrontation in the front room," Tah answered.

"We ganged up on her. She struck back. Any of us would have reacted the same way," Logan grunted.

"I—" Tah began, but Reno cut him off.

"He's right. We would have. We put her on the defensive from the beginning. We can't hold that against her now."

Tah sighed, but nodded in agreement with Reno. "You're right. Fuck, I feel like I'm making piss-poor decisions right now."

"We," Reno amended. "You're not in this alone."

Logan nodded his head in agreement.

"I will say this," Reno added. "I noticed, from the moment we met her in the woods, she defers to you. Hell, she dropped to her knees when she first saw you, and it wasn't to offer a blowjob."

Logan growled. He couldn't help it and refused to hold it in. Reno and Tah both looked at him. Reno's gaze went over him from head to toe. He inhaled deeply and shook his head.

"Have you mated her?" Reno asked bluntly.

"What?" Tah thundered.

"No," Logan answered with a shake of his head. "Not yet."

"Well, fuck," Tah muttered. He shrugged, rotated his head back and forth a few times then blew out a breath. "How did I miss that?"

"You've been a little preoccupied with Abby. And before you start beating yourself up, just stop. We'd be the same way in your place," Reno said. "But I'll be honest and say it was Amia who pointed the possibility out to me."

"Amia?" Logan questioned.

"She mentioned the way Clara took point in front of you when I shifted in the labs. Then how you pushed her behind you. Then when we were all talking to Clara, I noticed how pissed you were about it. You had your back against the wall, mad as hell. I imagine you were fighting a need to protect Clara," Reno said.

"I was," Logan agreed.

"But you haven't mated yet?" Tah asked.

"No. She's not ready. She's holding back, fighting the need building between us. I have no idea how, but she is," Logan admitted.

"And you? How are you holding up?" Reno asked.

"I'm one giant fucking boner," Logan said with a shaky laugh. "She's consumed my thoughts. I'm a walking hard-on, and she's the only cure. But the lady says no, and that's that."

"Maybe we should pull you from rotation," Tah said.

Logan snorted. "And replace me with who? Finn, Murphy and Zane are all still gone. We've got no one else."

"Speaking of them," Reno said, turning to Tah. "Have you heard from anyone?"

"No word from Finn still. I'm going to kick his ass when he gets back here for not answering. Zane checked in last night. They were following a trail into New Mexico. He didn't say much, just that they were still tracing Finn's steps and hoped to find him in the next day or two."

"But?" Logan asked. "I see the hesitation in your eyes, Tah. What's up?"

"I don't know. I just feel like Zane was holding something back. I got the feeling he didn't like something."

"So you think Zane and Murphy are keeping information from you? Why would they do that?" Reno asked.

"To protect the rest of us," Logan said. "Jesus! We need to stop trying to shield each other so much and start trusting each other to be able to deal with shit. This keeping stuff in order to protect each other is how people get killed."

"Do we go after them?" Reno asked.

"No," Tah said. "I can't risk it right now. I'm distracted with worry for Abby and the baby. Logan's distracted by Clara. We're already under-manned, and all of this isn't helping. We're going to have to trust Murphy, Finn and Zane to know what they're doing. I have to believe if they need us, they'll let us know."

Reno and Logan both nodded.

"So how do you want to handle talking to Clara?" Logan asked.

Tah sighed wearily. "Let's bring her in here. We'll keep it to the three of us for now. I'll talk to the Professor, see if he wants to join us. He's read all those journals just as Abby has. I'd prefer he be here instead of my mate," Tah admitted.

"I can't promise you Amia won't want to listen to what Clara has to say, and I won't keep anything from her," Reno said.

Tah sighed. "And what Amia knows, Abby knows."

"Afraid so," Reno admitted. "Those two are thick as thieves."

"It's a good thing," Logan stated. "I've noticed them with Kenzie. They seem to be bringing her out of her shell more. You know, in all the time we spent with the unit, how much do we know about Kenzie?"

"She doesn't have any family. She's quiet." Reno fired off a few things.

"She's a hell of a fighter," Tah added.

"But think about it. We all meshed together perfectly. We worked so well together that it made sense to call everyone in when this all went down. But other than their fighting abilities or weapon specialties, what do we know about Zane, Kenzie, Holt, Vic, Murphy or Finn?" Logan asked.

"You're right," Tah said. "We need to remedy that. If this is a pride, a family, then we need to act like one."

A knock on the door interrupted further conversation, especially when the Professor poked his head in. Seeing the three men inside, he seemed to think nothing of interrupting them. He just walked in, hands full of papers, glasses looking precariously close to falling off the end of his nose.

"Just who I've been looking for. Look at all this." He shook the papers, dropping a few onto the floor. "It's going to take weeks to go through all of this. I'd give them to Abby, but—" The Professor broke off at Tah's low rumble and shook his finger at the pride leader. "Don't take that tone with me, young man. I said I would, but she's in no state to be focusing on anything but the baby, and we all know it."

"What is all that?" Reno asked.

"More research, more information to sort through and see what answers we can find," the Professor mumbled. "And this isn't all of it. The printer was still spitting out pages when I left to find you."

"Where did you get it from?" Tah asked.

"Jess," the Professor said, and his eyes watered just a bit.

"Is she all right?" Reno asked immediately.

"She's fine. Still flitting here and there with those mates of hers on whatever quest they have." He wiped his eyes. "But you can't blame an old man for missing his only child every now and then."

"I'm sure she'd come visit again if you ask her to," Tah said.

The Professor shook his head. "She's a married woman now. Her mates come first."

"Not at the exclusion of you," Tah countered, and Logan wondered if he realized he was showing the affection he felt for the Professor.

The Professor shrugged off Tah's words. "This is all the information Jess had on hunters in general, and the Blanes, specifically. There's a lot to read through. It's going to take me a while."

"Amia and I can help," Reno offered.

"I just might take you up on that," the Professor said with a nod. "Diane offered to help, as well."

"Do you think the hunters have anything to do with what Jess and her wolves are dealing with?" Logan asked. If they were fighting the same battle, why not join forces?

The Professor looked thoughtful for a moment. "I think any shifter will always have to worry about hunters and people of their ilk. But I think whatever Jess and the boys are dealing with is more central to them."

"You don't know for sure?" Reno asked, echoing Logan's surprise.

"I know whatever it was, Jess and her mates faked my death to protect me from their enemies. Jess wouldn't tell me everything. My daughter has a need to protect those she loves."

"I can't imagine where she gets it from," Tah said.

The Professor smiled. "It was good hearing from her, even if it was only briefly. Now I better get back. I have a long night of reading ahead of me. And I want all of you down in the labs. I need some blood samples. Saliva, too."

They were all groaning when the Professor got to the door and turned back around. "I'll want some samples from Clara, as well. And Logan, I'll want another complete work-up on you in the next few days." With that parting shot, the Professor walked out, closing the door once more behind him.

"Fucking Vampire King," Logan muttered.

"I heard that, boy," the Professor called from the other side of the door. "Just get down to the labs before the end of the week and give me what I want."

Reno and Tah snickered as Logan went red.

"I swear he has ears like a bat," Logan grunted.

"A vampire bat," Reno said, and he and Tah started laughing again.

Logan shook his head but couldn't hold back a grin of his own. It was hard not to like the Professor, despite his constant harassing for blood. What the hell did he do with all that blood anyway?

* * * *

Murphy growled with frustration as he and Zane got back in the Jeep. Zane understood where his buddy was coming from. They should have caught up to Finn by now. Zane knew Murphy had a bad feeling deep in his gut. Murphy kept muttering about it every few minutes and rubbing at his skin as if he could feel something there. They needed to find Finn…soon.

"You sensing something?" Zane asked as he got behind the wheel. He'd taken over driving at the first stop, telling Murphy they wouldn't be able to help anyone if they were being scraped off the highway. Murphy was obviously so wrapped up in whatever he was intuiting in connection with his brother that he hadn't realized how fast he was going. They were damn lucky a cop hadn't come across their path.

"Relieved now that my bladder is empty," Murphy answered and Zane turned to stare at him.

"It unnerves me when you look at me that intensely. You're eyes are all weird, glowing yellow and shit," Murphy snapped. "So just ask what you want and let's go."

"I know you're getting antsy, and it seems to be getting worse. I won't be effective help if you keep me in the dark," Zane said. He ignored the jibe about his eyes. He'd heard some variation of it all his life. He didn't give a shit.

"I…I'm sorry, man," Murphy said with a grunt and shake of his head. "I have this really bad feeling, and I can't shake it. I can feel Finn in here." He thumped a fist against his chest. "I feel pain. God, my skin is fair to crawling with dread."

"You shouldn't have asked me not to say anything when I called Tah," Zane said with a grumble. "Especially knowing Finn was taken."

Murphy reluctantly nodded. "Someone took him at that spot where we found his phone outside of Santa Fe. Makes sense it was hunters following the signal the transmitter was putting out."

Neither of them mentioned the fact the device was turned off when Finn took it. It was understood Finn would have turned it back on as soon as he was far enough away from them. Zane just hoped they found Finn in time to tell him how stupid he was.

"The campsite we found. I could smell the mixture of scents there. Sweat laced with hate. Blood." Zane met Murphy's gaze without flinching. "You know what I am."

"I suspected," Murphy agreed with a nod. "What's your spirit?"

"Panther," Zane answered. "My uncle, too."

"Bet those eyes look just as eerie on a panther," Murphy said.

Zane paid no attention to the remark he was sure Murphy had intended to lighten the conversation. They were past that. There was heavy-duty shit going on. They needed honesty and communication. He was willing to hold some things back out of respect for the man he'd fought with as a Marine, but only if he knew why. "What I can't figure out is what your spirit is."

Murphy sighed. "Let's just focus on getting to Finn."

"You can't run forever," Zane warned. "At some point you have to claim a home. You know Tah will always see you as a member of this pride we're creating."

Murphy nodded. "I know, and I really hope to be a permanent part of it. But right now all I can think of is my brother out there. I promised to keep him safe. I promised."

"Talk to me, Murph," Zane pleaded as he started the engine and shifted into gear.

Murphy blew out a puff of air and finally began to talk. "Finn was born the same year I was. I came in January, and he followed in December. We've always been close."

"You're brothers," Zane said. "Family, and family guards each other's backs."

"Not always," Murphy muttered then shook his head as if that was something he didn't want to discuss.

Zane wondered at the story behind that comment.

"Finn decided he needed to look out for me," Murphy continued. "I kept telling him I was the older brother, and I was supposed to do the watching over. He never understood that."

"He took the transponder as much for you as to make amends to Reno and Amia," Zane stated. He'd wondered why Finn would feel the need to make amends like that. But protecting his brother? That was something Zane could definitely see Finn doing. Hell, the two brothers were always tripping over each other, trying to keep an eye out for the other.

Murphy nodded. "Probably more for me than to make any amends. He sees his actions as justifiable in the moment. As far as he's concerned, he did what he was told, and he refuses to believe anyone can hold a grudge when he pours on the Irish charm."

Zane smiled. That sounded just like the Finn he knew. "You Dockerys can be all charm when you want to."

"It's come in handy a time or two," Murphy said. "Finn has such an easy smile. He's always been a happy guy. Christ, I just want to see that grin of his again. Soon. And when I find him and know he's safe, I'm going to kick his fucking ass for putting me through this." Murphy gasped and grabbed his chest. "Ahhh, God. The pain. Jesus, my chest is burning."

"What's the matter?" Zane demanded, swerving to the side of the road.

"No," Murphy yelled. "Keep driving. I can sense him. God, my body feels like it's been set on fire. What are they doing to him? Jesus. What are they doing?"

"You're linked?"

Murphy groaned. "Yes. We have been since we were just boys. When I was..." He gritted his teeth and swallowed then started again. "When I was forced to leave, he came with me."

Zane said nothing for a while. He could tell Murphy wanted him to let it go, but he couldn't. He was keeping secrets from his alpha. The least Zane deserved was some honest answers. "What happened?" Zane asked long moments later.

"Hunters," Murphy said, his voice sounded bitter as if there was a hatred that burned deep inside him he couldn't contain.

"A Blane?" Zane questioned as things began to click into place in his head.

"No, but a hunter is a hunter," Murphy stated.

"That explains Finn's reaction to Amia. Why didn't you tell anyone you'd had a run in with hunters before? You know Tah needs information."

"And I have none, unless you want me to share what a body looks like when they're all done torturing it," Murphy snapped.

Zane glanced at him a few times before asking the question he knew Murphy was waiting for.

"Who?"

Murphy shut his eyes as if desperate to keep his memories at bay. "Christ, I see it every day as if it were just moments ago—red hair matted with blood. Green lifeless eyes. Limbs splayed at odd angles where bones had been broken then broken again. The smell of fear and pain and death. The hatred in my dad's eyes, mirrored in the stares of my two older brothers." He looked at Zane through the eyes of a man broken by tragedy. "Mum. They killed my mum, and I'll spend the rest of my life making sure every one of them pays for it." He gritted his teeth and jerked his head back, hissing out his breath while he pressed the heel of his hand against his chest. "Drive faster, Zane. I've got a really bad feeling."

Zane reached over and squeezed Murphy on the shoulder. "You're not alone anymore, Murphy. You or Finn. You have all of us, a new family, a pride. You need to let us in."

He put both hands on the wheel and drove as fast as he could. He wasn't much of a praying man, but he sent them out now with every mile they drove. *Please let us find Finn, and let him be alive.* He wasn't sure what Murphy would do if the worst happened. He wasn't sure what any of them would do.

Chapter Three

Clara was staring out the window when she heard the rattle of the door again. Logan must be coming back. She waited for his knock just so she could tell him to go away. And why did just the thought of seeing him have her pulse racing again? Instead, she heard a soft, tentative knock at the door.

"Clara, are you awake?"

It was Amia. Clara's pulse sped up for an entirely different reason this time. There were still so many secrets she didn't think she could share with Amia—secrets that weren't really hers to share with Amia. What if she slipped and said something? She could stir up even more trouble for herself. She could hurt Amia and Lydia and… Damn it! She really hated being swamped with uncertainty!

"Clara?" Amia called again, and Clara debated on pretending she was asleep just to avoid being alone with Amia. But that wasn't who Clara was, and she wasn't going to start now.

"I'm up," she called out. As bad as the idea probably was, she wanted to see Amia.

Amia pushed open the door and walked in as if they hadn't argued the last time they'd been together. Clara tensed, trying to prepare herself for whatever Amia felt the need to say when Amia took the wind out of her with two words.

"I'm sorry." Amia fidgeted with her pockets, looking uncomfortable.

"What?" Clara asked, unsure of why Amia was apologizing.

"For what happened downstairs. I'm the only one you know here. I should have stood beside you," Amia said, but she wasn't meeting Clara's eyes, making Clara question Amia's motives.

Lord, was she trying to put her own guilt on Amia now? The other woman had come in to apologize, and Clara was reading into it. She was utterly disgusted with herself.

"I let you suffer, did nothing to save you from the Blanes. I deserved to stand alone," Clara answered.

"No," Amia shook her head. "I might have thought that when I let pain and emotion influence me. But I know you did what you could. If you had tried to get me, they would have caught you and killed you. You said it, and you're right. I'm sorry, Clara."

"Don't say that. I don't deserve your forgiveness." God, if Amia only knew the secrets Clara held inside—secrets that belonged to the only mom she'd ever really known. Clara's dad had sent Lydia to them. He'd trusted her, and Clara was incapable of not doing the same. Trusting and loving Lydia no matter what the cost.

"It's mine to give, regardless. And I'm giving it."

Clara watched as Amia stepped farther into the room and sat cross-legged at the foot of the bed. "We've gone about things all wrong. God, you caught us at a rough point. But I'm guessing there will always be something going on here."

"You mean the tracker they put in you?"

Amia nodded. "Tracker, transponder, whatever you want to call it. I'm lucky they didn't locate me here. I could have gotten everybody killed."

Clara saw the horror in Amia's eyes and moved to sit beside her. "Don't torture yourself like that. None of this is your fault."

"I'm a Blane."

The words softly spoken hit Clara hard. It was like stepping into the past and listening to Lydia finally confess who she was. She'd give Amia the same words now that she'd given to Lydia then.

"You're just as much a victim in all of this as anyone," Clara countered. "Probably more so."

"I wish I'd known you were watching me. It would have been nice to have a friend," Amia whispered, and Clara felt her heart ache.

What would Amia say if she knew Clara had once pretended Amia was her sister?

"I've never really had a friend, either," Clara admitted.

"Really? I just assumed you must have grown up in a pride with lots of others around," Amia said.

Clara shook her head. "We took in a random stray or two, but most never stayed. I had my uncle, though."

"And your adopted mom," Amia added.

Clara swallowed, feeling a little sick at the continued deceit. "Yes, and her."

"I guess I was envisioning a huge pride."

"People tend to trickle in and out. We're a refuge for those in need. Some stay, but most move on eventually. We've managed to build a network of sorts, though," Clara confessed.

"We could really use your help here," Amia told her.

"I already told Logan I'd tell all of you what I could about the hunters and the Blane family," Clara said.

"We're not the enemy, Clara, though I know we've done a really bad job of showing you that. I hate seeing you locked in here, looking so sad. Damn it! I'm saying something to Tah about this. It's not right. You've done nothing wrong," Amia muttered angrily.

"I followed you here, and Reno's right. I wanted to be found. This might not be what I was after, but I put myself in this situation," Clara countered. "I let anger rule me when we were talking. I said things I shouldn't have."

"The story you told Abby? About the baby?" Amia asked.

"Better to warn her now than to tell pretty lies. Lies don't save lives," Clara retorted. She took a deep breath and shook her head. She was reacting with anger again, and that wasn't how she wanted to continue. Her tone was softer when she spoke again. "I don't want to see her suffer like that."

"It wasn't just a story, was it?" Amia asked.

Clara dropped her head to her chest and closed her eyes as the past come rushing back. "No."

"What happened?" Amia asked softly. "Who? Was it your mother?"

"My aunt."

"Did you…" Amia swallowed audibly, and Clara looked up and met her gaze.

"Yes, I saw it happen. My uncle and dad were gone. I was staying with my Aunt Stella. They were expecting their first baby. Uncle Thomas was so excited. He'd croon to Aunt Stella's belly. It made me laugh to see them."

"How old were you?" Amia asked.

"Five," Clara answered. She could still smell the cookies in the air. They'd been baking. Happy and carefree. The next minute Aunt Stella had stilled and told Clara to go to the safe room.

"Did…did they hurt you?"

"No. I was in the safe room. She sent me there, planning to follow, but they were quicker than she'd expected. She never made it." Clara stood again and walked to the window, wrapping her arms around her waist to try to keep herself from shaking apart. "I saw the whole thing on one of the monitors my dad had installed."

"Oh, my God. You were only five!" Amia exclaimed.

"The hunter doesn't distinguish between male or female, adult or child. I'm sure you saw that, Amia." She turned to glance at the other woman. "Even if you don't want to believe you did. All they see is the animal. All they feel is a need to rip it out and kill it."

"Clara—" Amia began.

"Do not tell me you're sorry. You made the choice to save, Amia. That's who you are. Not a hunter, no matter your last name." Just like your mother, she wanted to add, but held the words inside, unspoken. She turned back to look out the window and caught a glimpse of Logan. As if he felt her eyes on him, he glanced up. It was like a jolt of electricity passed between them, igniting a fiery lust inside her that never seemed to die away. She wouldn't be able to deny him much longer. He was her mate. They were meant to be.

"Were they Blanes? The ones who killed your aunt?" Amia asked.

"Doesn't matter," Clara told her.

"Yes, it does."

"No," Clara turned and faced Amia with exasperation. "That's what you're not getting. It doesn't matter. All that matters is that it was a hunter. It was a hunter that held her down while another cut her open and ripped my unborn cousin from her womb. It was a hunter who took pleasure in making her watch as they did things to her child no mother should ever have to endure. And it was a hunter who left her there to bleed out and die. It doesn't matter what their goddamned last names were."

"Oh, God." Amia covered her mouth with her hand.

"I know you of all people are aware of the cruelty of hunters. There's no way you didn't see it all around you when you were growing up," Clara said.

"Marcus kept me in the house. I wasn't allowed in the yard unless he was there. I was kept away from most of it," Amia admitted.

"Why? Why would he do that?" Clara demanded.

"I don't know. He just did. I always thought he was waiting for me to betray him the way my mother did."

Clara quieted, trying to decide how to approach this topic. "How did your mother betray him?" she finally asked.

"I don't know. I just know she did. No one was ever allowed to speak of her after she died, especially me."

"She died?"

Amia nodded. "Marcus burned all her stuff. He told me to be good and remember my place or I'd be joining her. I think… I think he might have killed her."

Clara held her breath. Now was the perfect time to confess the truth. All she had to do was open her mouth and tell Amia the truth

Your mother's alive. She's alive and has been living with me this whole time.

But Clara couldn't tell. She'd given her word to her Uncle Thomas, and he was one person she would do her best not to let down.

"You were the first person I saw dragged in by hunters since I was a little girl. Once I saw you, I couldn't look away. There was something about you that drew me to you," Amia continued.

"You saw the glow of the animal inside me. It's a hunter gift, but you've used it for good," Clara said.

"I knew I couldn't let you die. I made my choice that night. They were getting ready to train me. Marcus and Kellan had some plan to marry me off to Kellan." Amia shuddered and Clara knew the other woman was imagining what life would have been like then.

"You both have the gift of sight. They probably hoped any children you had would have the same."

"I don't care. I'm just glad I got the hell out of there. Betrayal kept Kellan from having me. I'll take the scars. Seems like a good trade to me."

"You do realize what this means," Clara prompted Amia.

"What? You think they'll still come after me?"

Clara shrugged. "I don't know on that. It depends on how obsessed Marcus is with you, I guess. I was referring to what it could mean for you and Reno, for the pride."

"What?"

"You could have the first shifter born with the gift of sight," Clara said. "Not that we need it to sense who is and who isn't. But wouldn't that be a slap in the face to every hunter out there. A shifter born with a hunter's sight."

Amia grinned. "It would. It's almost enough to make me want to have Reno's baby."

"You don't want kids?"

"Not now," Amia said. "Seeing how much Abby's pregnancy is taking out of her. God! It terrifies me to watch her getting weaker and weaker every day."

"Why is she weakening? Is there something wrong with the baby?"

"Not that any of Diane's equipment shows. Baby looks strong and healthy. But it's growing so fast. Abby's body can't seem to handle it," Amia said.

"I don't understand. Was Abby sick before she became pregnant?"

"No. From what she said, she's rarely ever sick."

"Then the pregnancy shouldn't be harming her. She's taking vitamins?"

"Yes," Amia said with a nod.

"Getting plenty of rest and not overdoing it?"

"She isn't allowed to do much anymore. But she's not resting. She's exhausted. Her body aches all the time."

“I don’t understand. Each transfusion should reinvigorate her and help her body adapt to the changes the baby is making.”

“Transfusion?”

“Oh, God! I didn’t think. He’s…” She cut herself off. “I just expected you guys to know. God, this is all so complicated.”

“What transfusions?” Amia demanded again.

“Abby needs a transfusion of Tah’s blood. His child. His blood. All it takes is a pint every few weeks, and her body will be fine. My God! She hasn’t had any transfusions? How far along is she?”

“Almost twelve weeks.”

“Jesus. She’s a hell of woman to survive what her body is going through with no shifter blood given to her. Twelve weeks. Holy shit! The baby will be here in just a few more weeks.”

“You know about pregnancy?” Amia asked.

“Yes,” Clara answered. “My mother died giving birth to me. We didn’t know anything then. When I was just a baby, a shifter came through. He taught my uncle and his best friend a lot of things we didn’t know, especially when it came to medicine and pregnancy. As soon as she gets the blood, she’ll feel a difference within an hour or so.”

“Thank you, Clara. Thank you so much. You’ve just given us the greatest information of all. Tah will give you anything for this. If this helps Abby…”

“It will. I promise. Now go! The sooner they give it, the sooner she’ll feel better.”

Amia turned to head out of the room then surprised Clara by turning back to her and hugging her. There was a look in her eyes, one of such confliction that Clara was jolted by it.

“You may have just saved Abby’s life. There are no words to tell you how much this means.”

“Go,” Clara urged as emotions tumbled through her, emotions she didn’t want to face. She turned her head to the side and glanced around the room, anywhere but at the woman hugging her.

With that one word Amia turned and hurried out of the room.

“Wait!” Clara called, but the door had clicked shut, the lock reengaging and preventing Clara from going after Amia. She reached on the bed and picked up what Amia had left behind. "You forgot your phone."

Clara looked at the phone. Did she dare? It would probably be a while before Amia noticed and came back for it. If Clara erased the number as soon as the call ended, it would be okay. She really wanted to hear her uncle's voice. The question was whether using the phone was a risk she was willing to take.

* * * *

Logan was talking to Tah and Reno when Amia rushed down the hall past them heading toward the stairs to the lab.

"Tah!" she cried out. "Follow me. Now."

"What is it?" Tah roared. "Abby!"

He tore past her, screaming his mate's name as he went.

"What happened?" Reno asked as he and Logan came up behind Amia.

"It's good news, I swear," she panted.

"What's going on?" Abby demanded as they hit the bottom of the stairs.

Logan noticed again how pale and frail she looked. The vibrant Abby was fading fast.

"Amia, you scared Tah to death. And he scared Diane and me with all his shouting. My God, I thought more hunters were here."

Logan saw it then, the shadow of what Clara had told her in Abby's eyes. Now he understood Tah's anger. It still didn't sit well with Logan. It beat against his need to protect Clara.

"Sorry," Amia said, catching her breath. "I was with Clara."

"Is she all right? Did you hurt her?" Logan demanded.

"Calm down, Logan," Reno said, moving to block Logan's access to Amia.

Fuck. Logan was so focused on Clara he hadn't even realized he'd moved threateningly toward Amia.

"She's fine. She told me why Abby is getting weak. I know what we need to do."

"What?" Diane demanded. "Tell me."

"Clara said Abby needs a transfusion of Tah's blood. She should have been getting them every few weeks. His child. His blood. It will strengthen her and allow her body to adapt to all the changes taking place," Amia told them. "Shifter child. Shifter blood."

"Into the lab," Diane ordered Abby and Tah. "I'll get the equipment set up."

"Do you think she's telling us the truth?" Abby asked, holding back when everyone around her was ready to rush.

"She wouldn't lie to you, Abby," Logan admonished. "Not even to keep you from hating her."

Tah growled, but Logan just turned to look at him, not willing to back down even for Abby. Clara was his mate, whether they'd consummated it or not.

"It wasn't just a story she told you," Amia said softly, and Logan turned to look at her just as everyone else did. "Clara saw it happen to her aunt. She was five years old and had to witness something that horrific. We all have our demons, Abby. You, me and Clara."

"Jesus," Tah said, looking a little sick.

Amia looked at Logan. "She was buried alive as well. It's where she was when I went to find her the night we escaped. She was chained to the wall. They—"

"Don't." Logan stopped her. "Haven't we put her through enough?"

Amia nodded. Abby's cheeks were wet with tears. Reno clasped Logan's arm and gave it a squeeze.

"Go to her," Tah told him. "Claim your mate."

"Set her free, Logan," Amia said. "I think she lets her demons control her as much as I did. Set her free the way Reno did me."

And they paired off before him. Tah with his arm around Abby, and Reno clasping Amia close to his side. That's what Logan wanted for him and Clara. He wanted that unwavering bond. He wanted Clara to know that he was hers—that he would watch over and protect her for the rest of their lives. Hell, if she gave him the chance, he was willing to bet he'd fall head over heels in love with her. He was her mate. All she had to do was claim him.

Chapter Four

Clara stared at the phone for a long time before finally giving in. She swiped her finger across the screen to see if it was passcode-protected. It wasn't. It came alive in her hand and the little phone icon was right there. It felt as if it was jumping up and down, waving at her, and shouting here I am, come and use me. Just a phone call.

She heard the lock and looked around frantically. Was it Amia? Was she coming back for the phone already? She scurried to the bed and stuck it between the mattress and box springs. First place most people would look, but it was the best she could do. Then she felt stupid and guilty, conflicted. She shouldn't be hiding a damn phone.

Logan pushed the door wide and stood there looking at her for the longest moment, and the phone left her thoughts completely.

"What?" Clara caught her bottom lip between her teeth as she bounced her gaze over him then around the room, looking for any reason as to why he was staring at her with such fixation.

Logan didn't say a word. He carefully shut the door and turned to face her, grabbing her attention and holding it as he started toward her. She hadn't realized she was backing away from him until she felt the wall behind her. He stopped inches in front of her and leaned in until there was nothing but their breath between them.

"Logan?"

"You are the most remarkable woman."

"Okay..." Clara wasn't sure how to respond to that. What was he talking about? There was only one thing she could figure he was alluding to. "Is this about the information I gave Amia to help Abby?"

"Your help might just eliminate the biggest strain on our pride right now."

"I'm sorry. I didn't think about you not knowing what to do. The transfusions are a must to help during pregnancy."

"Diane is taking care of it now."

"I'm glad I could help."

"I watched them down there. Tah and Abby. Reno and Amia. Friends, lovers, mates. I thought to myself, this is what Clara and I could have."

"Logan."

His name was a moan as he skimmed his lips along her jaw line up toward her ear.

"I'm tired of being alone. Not when I know I don't have to be anymore. Not when I know my mate is right here, wanting me just as fiercely. Why are you denying us?" He rocked into her, letting her feel the bulge of his cock. He pressed it right between her thighs and rocked again, lifting her up on her toes. "Why deny this?"

She was asking herself the same question. Her uncle would expect her to be smart, to be safe, but he would never ask her to shut out or walk away from a mate. Mates were what kept them going—the quest to find them, the instinct to keep them safe and happy, and the desire to avenge them. Mates were the lifeblood of a shifter. What was she doing trying to deny herself?

She gripped his shoulders and leapt up until she could wrap her legs around his waist. Her turn to take control and show him what she wanted. She rotated her hips and ground her pussy against the swell of his cock.

"Be warned. If I claim you, you're mine. I won't let you go. I won't be able to. You will become a part of me, always."

"Same goes, baby. You'll be mine, all mine, and I don't share. I'll be hard-pressed not to kill anyone who tries to come between us."

She bent low and nipped his bottom lip. "Nothing will come between us. Be sure, Logan. Be very sure." She knew the agony one mate went through when they lost the other. She'd seen it with her Uncle Thomas. She'd glimpsed it in her father's eyes.

He turned quickly and took her down on the bed. His hips pressed hers into the mattress, but he used his hands to keep his chest above her. He stared down at her, checks flushed and eyelids at half-mast.

"Does it feel like I'm unsure?"

"Mating is more than sex."

"I'm counting on it."

Before she could say anything else, he rubbed his lips over hers. He kissed both corners of her mouth and ran his tongue over the seam until she parted them with a gasp. She wrapped her hands around his head, burying her fingers in the thick strands of his sandy brown hair. He pressed his tongue inside and she met him, rubbing his tongue with hers, leading it farther into her mouth. She sucked at him, loving the deep groan he gave and the way his hips pumped restlessly against her.

"I need to be inside you," Logan panted out as he broke from the kiss. His lips skimmed over her as if he were unable to stop tasting her skin.

"I want to taste you," she countered, trying to use her purchase in his hair to urge him back up to her kiss.

"Later," he promised as he licked and sucked along the column of her neck, heading lower. He glanced up at her. "This is just our first mating, not our only."

"Yes." She moaned as he captured the rigid point of her nipple through her shirt and sucked on it. He nipped it with his teeth then pulled away to move to the other one.

"I need you naked." He grunted. "Now."

He moved back and gripped the neck of her shirt, ripping it wide and exposing her black cotton bra.

"God, I knew you would be perfection."

"Wait!" she cried.

He hung his head and breathed roughly through his nose. He rolled off of her and lay beside her on the bed, one arm thrown over his eyes. "You changed your mind."

"What?" Clara sat up. "No."

He moved his arm to look at her. "You said wait."

Clara stood up and moved between his knees where they rested on the edge of the bed. She nudged his feet a little farther apart on the floor and grinned down at him. "I just didn't want you to rip the rest of my clothes off. I have a limited wardrobe here, and I didn't see a clothing store hidden in the trees out there."

Logan lifted up on his elbows as she popped the button on her pants and slid the zipper down. "There's a town close by. I'll buy you anything you want."

She grinned. "You're supposed to offer gifts before you get the prize."

"Every time with you will be a prize."

Her eyes went misty. "I know so little about you. God, practically nothing. But I see the way you care about those around you. I see the way you treat people, and it tells me you're a good man."

"I hadn't thought of that. I've been so consumed with this intense need for you that I never stopped to think that we know very little about one another."

"It's the biological factor of mating. When a shifter finds their mate, the need to claim them is overwhelming. My Uncle Thomas said most believe it stems from a need to continue our species. But a mate isn't just some random person. It's the person genetically equipped to procreate with you."

"Got that covered." Logan sat up and pulled a condom out of his pocket. "I wouldn't forget. I'd never do that to you. The last thing we need is you getting pregnant."

"You don't want kids?" Clara asked and felt her heart breaking a bit.

Procreation wasn't something she could control. Birth control didn't usually work for them. They could try a condom, but she had to make sure he understood it might not work for them. In males, it had to do with the physical changes that took place with the penis during the time when his mate was most fertile. For females, her body would produce a unique hormone that would create sensitivity to anything between them. It would physically cause pain for him to wear a condom. Plus the need would be so high, they'd be lucky to leave the bedroom.

"I'd love to have kids," Logan said, interrupting her thoughts. "But you just reminded us we have a lot to learn about one another. Plus, I've seen what Abby has been going through. I wouldn't be able to handle seeing you suffer like that."

Clara smiled. "It's not the same for female shifters carrying young. I'm the shifter so I already make the blood required to carry a shifter baby to term. I'll be fine. Abby's dilemma lays in the fact she's human. I know of a lot of shifters who lost mates before we were given the information on transfusions."

"I'd like to hear about that." He shook his head. "Not about those who lost loved ones. But about how it was growing up. The things you said in that room. You've had a rough life."

"No rougher than what others have been through," she answered with a shrug. "I had my uncle, so I had the gift of being around someone who loves me. That's a lot to be grateful for in the grand scheme of things."

He nodded. "You're right."

"Logan." She shoved her jeans down, loving the way his breath caught while he watched. "We don't need a condom. I can't get pregnant unless I'm in heat, which only happens in my fertile time. Trust me when I tell you, you won't have to ask when that happens. Your body will know."

Logan grinned. "I saw the way Tah and Abby were during that time. Can't say I'm not looking forward to all that sex."

She stepped out of her pants and kicked them aside. "I also can't contract any form of STD, which means I can't carry them, either. So you're safe with me."

"I'm clean. The military checks, and I haven't been with anyone since I got out."

"A sexy guy like you?"

"Maybe I knew I was waiting for you," he quipped, but there was sincerity in his eyes.

She reached around and began unhooking her bra while he watched. "I want to know everything there is to know about you. Later." She shrugged her straps down her arms and tossed the bra aside. She cupped her breasts, running her fingertips over her straining nipples while she glanced at him. "Much later. Right now, I really want to feel you."

"Sweet Jesus, I want to feel you, too." His control seemed to snap as he reached for her and tugged her closer between his sprawled legs. His mouth was even with her breast with him sitting on the side of the bed. "Let me taste you," he purred.

She moved her fingers and offered her turgid nipple to him. He latched on and sucked ravenously, pulling it up toward the roof of his mouth where he played with it with his tongue. His hands found her ass, squeezing and fondling her rounded cheeks. He released her nipple and blazed a path of sinful greed to the other one. Clara was on fire. She wanted more than his mouth, more than his hands, and she wanted to do some tasting of her own.

"Take…yours…off…" she panted as he continued to torment her with pleasure.

His hands dropped from her ass, and she heard the rip of material as he spread his shirt wide and shrugged it off his shoulders. He caught her nipple with his teeth and gave it a hard nip before letting her go. He grabbed her waist and swung her around as he stood so that she landed on her knees on the bed.

"My turn to strip," he said, already reaching for the belt on his jeans. "Maybe you should lose the panties while I do. I'd hate to rip them. They're sexy."

"Got a thing for black cotton?" she asked with a laugh. Her panties were functional but not sexy.

"I've got a thing for anything when it's on you."

His eyes were molten chocolate as he spoke, and she knew he meant it. The rasp of his zipper sliding down had her gaze skimming over his broad shoulders and following the sprinkling of hair across his muscular chest down over his well-defined abs and lower to the band of his underwear that she could just see. Mother of all that was sacred! He was delicious. And hers, all hers.

She dipped her hand inside the front of her panties and slid her fingers between her damp lips to her core. Thrusting two fingers in, she stroked herself while she enjoyed the show of him undressing. She loved the way his nostrils flared and eyelids dipped as he took in what she was doing.

"Jesus, Clara. You're going to make me come just watching you."

"Want me to stop?" she asked and teased him by removing her hand. Her fingers were damp from her juices, and she slowly began lifting them toward her mouth.

He intervened, snatching her hand mid-air and carrying it to his lips instead. He sucked both fingers into his mouth and moaned with pure pleasure.

"I want to gorge myself on your sweet pussy," he crooned, flicking his tongue over her fingers again and again.

She slid her other hand down inside his jeans and cupped his taut balls before walking her fingers up his rigid shaft. "I'd like to gorge myself, as well."

"Fuck!" He shifted, spreading his legs a bit wider as she stroked him through his underwear.

"Or we could do that," she agreed.

"Clothes," Logan muttered, easing her hand out of his fly and taking a step back. "Off. Now."

She shimmied her panties down her hips and thighs until they caught on her knees. She sat back and swung her legs around in front of her to finish wiggling out of them. Her eyes never left Logan the whole time. He kicked off his shoes then shoved his jeans and sexy trunk briefs to his ankles in one move. He bent to tug off his socks with the rest of it and hid his hard cock from her avid gaze. Not that the rest of him wasn't beautiful, but she really wanted to see what she'd only felt against her so far, especially since his clothing was gone.

He stood, and Clara caught her breath, licking her lips as her mouth seemed to go dry. His erection was long and thick, curving a bit in the center. The head crowned over the shaft, already damp with pre-cum she was dying to taste.

"Come here," she crooned, turning onto her hands and knees and crawling to the side of the bed in front of him. "Let me taste. Just a little taste."

He groaned but complied, stepping closer until his cock hung just inches away from her moist lips. She leaned in and flattened her tongue over him, licking up and around, taking the drop of fluid with her.

"Mhmm." She moaned and swirled her tongue around the head. "You taste sweet with just a hint of spice. I could suck you for hours." She wrapped her lips around him and twirled her mouth over the head and down the shaft, taking as much of him as she could.

"Easy," he warned, reaching down and grabbing his dick. He eased it from her lips with a pop since she refused to quit sucking. "I'm already on the edge, baby. I want inside you."

She raised her gaze to meet his. "Just tell me how you want me."

He growled. "Jesus, that's a loaded question."

Clara laughed. "The offer stands."

"On your back. I want to see your eyes. I want to lose myself in you."

"You say the best things." She rose up on her knees and jerked him to her, taking his mouth and pulling him under with her. She wrapped her arms around his shoulders, tugging him down with her as she sat back and moved to recline.

He dropped his hands to the bed to keep his weight off of her as she maneuvered her legs, then continued following her as she eased farther back on the bed. He moved his legs between hers, and grunted when she automatically lifted them to grip his hips. He went down on his left elbow and moved his right hand lower to rub between her pussy lips. She knew he could tell how wet and ready she was.

He thrust two fingers deep, and they both groaned.

"Fuck me, Logan," she begged.

He slid his fingers free and reached for his dick. She stared at him as he guided it to her pussy and pressed into her. He was slow and easy, taking his time as he possessed her this first time.

"Logan." She called his name, needing him to look into her eyes while he claimed her. There would be time for them to watch the joining of their bodies later.

He met her gaze again as if he knew what she wanted. A smile tugged at his lips then his eyes closed and she could see the pleasure wash over him as he thrust deep inside her. It was perfect, as if they had been designed just for each other. He rocked into her, penetrating deep before pulling back until only the tip remained. Again and again.

It was amazing how attuned to one another they were. She'd heard that sex was different when you found your mate, that it was a shared pleasure beyond anything you could imagine. They were right, so right. She might not know Logan the way normal relationships progressed. There'd been no dates or 'get-to-know-you-better' sessions where they discussed favorite colors or foods. But their bodies knew each other—their souls accepted without question that they were destined to be together.

Logan leaned down and sipped from her lips. "Take me while I take you." He turned his head slightly, offering her the perfect spot to claim him. "Make me yours as I make you mine."

She lifted her head and nuzzled the skin where the strong column of his neck met the broad shelf of his shoulder. She inhaled the spicy musk of his skin, licked over his flesh and tasted the sweet essence of him. He fucked her harder, faster, urging her without words to do what he wanted. She grazed her teeth over him, knowing this one act would bind them together for the rest of their lives. Even after death.

She glanced up to see his gaze fixed on her, watching as she caressed his skin.

"Are you sure?" she asked. There would be no going back after this, for either of them.

"I've been sure since the first moment I saw you. One look, and I knew you were my future, the missing piece I've waited my whole life to find."

She sunk her teeth deep, tasting the metallic flavor of his blood and sucking it in. She knew her saliva would be working its way into his bloodstream. It would begin making minor changes in him, linking them together while enhancing his senses and allowing his body to create antibodies that allowed for faster healing. They would be one, even when they weren't together. They would feel the other, sense if something was wrong or if the other was in danger. It would only grow stronger with each passing day. It was the way with mated couples.

He fucked her hard and fast, pounding his thick cock in and out. She pulled her teeth free and licked over the wound she'd made.

"Yes! God, yes!" she cried against his skin.

"Come for me," Logan commanded and slid his hand back down between them.

She felt the brush of his fingers over her distended clit and bucked up into him.

"That's it, baby. Come all over my dick."

"Ahhh," she screamed as she jerked against him. She could feel her juices spilling around his shaft as she did as he commanded.

Logan dropped his head to her neck and gripped her trapezius muscle with his teeth. It was a sign of dominance, one she would accept from no man, save her mate. Only he would be able to persuade her to back down from something. She would always show deference to her alpha, but Tah would never hold the power her mate would. Did Logan know that? Did he have any idea the influence he had when it came to her?

He released her with a cry, his head thrown back as he roared in orgasm. She felt the hot wash of his seed filling her and clung to him, flying high into ecstasy with him. And for the first time in her life, she felt completely free. She wasn't a daughter, a niece, a rescuer or a watcher. She was simply Clara, Logan's mate. It was the most liberating sensation in the world.

Logan collapsed on top of her, pinning her to the bed under him as they both fought to get oxygen in. He turned to glance at her and jerked up so quickly she cried out.

"Fuck!" he exclaimed, moving off of her and running his hands over her. "Did I hurt you? Where? Shit, Clara, I didn't mean to. I swear."

"What?" She shook her head, a little dazed. "You didn't hurt me. Why would you think that?"

He swiped a finger under her eye and came away with moisture. "You're crying."

"I am?" She put her hands to her face and felt the tears covering her cheeks. "I didn't realize…"

"Are you okay?"

She nodded her head. "Hold me?"

"Always." He lay back down next to her and tugged her over until her head was on his chest. He had one arm under her, the other was brushing through her disheveled hair. "I've got you."

"Don't let go, Logan. Promise me you won't let me go."

"Never," he vowed, and she believed him.

There was so much they hadn't spoken of that they were going to have to. She had no idea how the rest of the pride would react to finding out Lydia Blane was still alive and well. How would it affect Amia? Would it turn everyone against Clara for good? If it didn't and she stayed, would she be able to work with Tah without insulting him with what she knew and he didn't? God, what a mess!

She needed to make a call, and get some answers herself. Then maybe she could handle all of this without fucking everything up and creating discord where they needed an alliance.

Chapter Five

"So tell me about your family," Clara urged Logan.

"This is it," he said. "All the people here. These are my family."

"What about outside of here? Your parents? Siblings?"

He sighed and began stroking her hair through his fingers. "I haven't seen my parents in a long time. My dad was very set against me becoming a Marine. He gave me an ultimatum. I chose the Marines."

"Why? If your family was so against it?"

"Defiance. Arrogance. Who knows? By the time I turned eighteen I was so ready to get out of that house and out from under his thumb, I would have done anything he told me not to."

"Doesn't sound like you had a great childhood," Clara whispered.

"It was all right. He wasn't abusive or anything like that. I never wanted for anything. We butted heads a lot. He had his way of wanting things, and I went about it just the opposite."

"What about your mother?"

Logan shrugged. "Mom always sided with Dad on everything. What he said was the law, and that was that as far as she was concerned."

"Any brothers or sisters?"

"I have a younger sister, Laura."

"Do you ever talk to her?"

"I haven't spoken to anyone since I left. I wrote a few letters home at first, but no one ever answered."

"Your family sucks, Logan."

His laughter tickled her ear. "No. My family's the people here, the ones I chose and who chose me. Tah and Reno. Finn and Murphy. Zane, Holt, Vic and Kenzie. We became a family when we were in the same unit. I know I can trust all of them with my life. Now I have Abby and Amia, the Professor and Diane." He tipped her chin up so she met his gaze. "And you. Now I have you. I'd say my life is pretty wonderful now."

She shook her head. "Now your life is shifters and the hunters who feel it's their job to rid the world of the abomination we are. They won't ever stop, and it won't matter if you're human or not. You've mated me. To them you've chosen a side and that makes you fair game as far as they're concerned."

"Let them come. We'll stop them just like we did the last time."

"How many hunters did you face last time? A half dozen? A dozen? Or a fully equipped team?"

"We stopped them. It doesn't matter how many they send. We'll keep stopping them." She felt him rubbing at his chest and took a closer look at the scar she'd noticed earlier.

"You were shot," she stated.

Logan nodded. "The hunters used a type of stink bomb. We were all out in the woods. The Professor's daughter Jess and her mates were here. They were working with Tah, trying to teach him how to shift."

"Is she the one I heard was mated to the four alpha wolves?"

Logan grinned. "Sounds a little crazy, I know. But they all seem pretty happy."

"I won't share you like that," Clara declared with narrowed eyes.

"I don't share," Logan replied, flipping them so that she lay under him on the bed. "You're all mine, Clara. My woman. My mate."

She let the joy his words brought her show on her face. "I like the sound of that."

"I'd keep you in this bed indefinitely and keep showing you, but you really need to talk to Tah. There's so much we need to learn from you."

"There are a few things I should tell you first."

"Like what?"

"Now that we've mated, you'll notice a few changes."

"The enhanced senses and all that," he said with a nod. "And I'll get that super cool healing buff. Gotta admit, I'm going to love that."

"There's more than those," she said with a smile. "We'll be joined now. Here." She moved her hand from his heart to hers. "Linked. Soon, I'll know if you're in danger and vice versa. I'll sense your emotions as you'll sense mine. I won't know what you're thinking," she said, noting the look in his eyes.

"You're misreading me if you think I'm concerned about that. I'm an open book. If I'm pissed, you'll know it. Luckily, I rarely get that way. I'm more concerned with you being okay with me being able to pick up on what you're feeling."

"You're my mate," she said with a shrug. "I'm just sorry that I'm so uncertain right now. I'm usually not this way. Following Amia and finding all of you. It's thrown me for a loop."

"We're on your side," he assured her. "There's nothing to be afraid of."

"Didn't seem that way when I was being interrogated." She pressed her fingers to his lips when he started to speak. "I'm sorry about that. I shouldn't have said it. It doesn't matter anymore. That was then. We're mated now, and I know I won't stand alone again."

"Never," he swore.

"The truth is, I'm uncertain of what to say to Tah. There's so much information that none of you seem to know. I don't feel adequately prepared to share it all. I really think it would be best coming from an older and wiser shifter."

"Your uncle?"

"Yes, he'd be a great person to talk to." She nodded vigorously. "If you'd just persuade Tah to let me call him. Tah or you can be there when I do if he's concerned with what I might say or do. I won't betray this pride. I wouldn't betray you, ever."

"I know that."

"Which means I need to tell you that Amia left her phone in here when she hurried out earlier. I thought about making a call but didn't. It's under the mattress."

Logan pushed up and rose from the bed. "I'll grab my phone and give it to you. Things have changed now. You're my mate. That makes you part of this pride."

"I have a phone I can use. It's hidden in the woods with the rest of my stuff. I just haven't had a chance to go get it, yet."

"I'll take you. I'm curious to see where you hid it. We've been all over the woods and found nothing."

"I'll show you."

He reached down and took her hand, tugging her up. "Time to get up and dressed."

"Logan." She said his name quietly when he moved to rummage on the floor for their clothing.

"I'll give you one of my shirts to wear for now," he said, turning back to her as he sorted what he'd picked up. "It's going to be huge. Sorry about that."

"Logan," she said again.

"Yeah?"

"It was a hunter who shot you, wasn't it?"

He nodded, absently reaching up to rub the scar he'd always bear.

"Is he still living?"

Logan shook his head. "Reno killed him."

"Good," she said with a nod. "I hope he ripped his fucking heart out."

Logan grinned. "Bloodthirsty, aren't you?"

"No one will ever threaten my man. You are mine, and I protect what's mine."

He jerked her up against him and took her mouth in a savage kiss. It was wild heat and unbridled passion. His tongue ravaged the interior of her mouth, owning her. She nipped his bottom lip hard enough to draw blood, tasting it on her tongue as he pulled back. His hand fisted in her hair as he held her in place.

"You're mine, Clara. You will never place yourself in front of me when there is danger. I protect what's mine. I won't deny you the fight, but don't ever think to try and deny me, either."

"By your side," she vowed. "Always."

He nodded, loosening his grip until he cupped the back of her skull. He guided her mouth back to his, the kiss soft and lazy this time. She knew he was remembering that moment in the lab when she'd tried to place herself between him and Reno. In her defense, Reno had been a fully shifted tiger at the time, and she'd taken one look at Logan and felt the mating call scream through her. She'd been completely off-guard in that split second with only one thought in mind. Protecting her mate.

"I'll go grab you a shirt," he said as he slowly eased away from her. "Then we'll go talk to Tah and get your gear."

"The phone call?" she asked.

"You'll get to make it. I'll make sure Tah doesn't have a problem with it," Logan assured her. "He'll understand where your loyalty lies now that we're mated."

She watched Logan pull up his jeans and turn to leave the room. Where her loyalties lay? Not as easy a question as Logan seemed to think. Yes, she was loyal to her mate and understood that, as such, she would be expected to show loyalty to his pride. But that didn't mean she could just turn her back on her uncle and the shifters that stayed with them. And Lydia? What about her? How did she tell Amia that Lydia was alive and well and had been living with shifters this whole time? Clara was Logan's mate, but that didn't make everything else magically disappear.

"What do I do?" she whispered, praying for some divine guidance since she didn't have a clue.

Logan ran into Tah in the hallway. Tah inhaled deeply and sighed.

"I see you took my advice and mated Clara."

"Yes," Logan confirmed. "She's mine, Tah. I did what our hormones have been demanding of us. I know you remember how this mating thing consumes you."

Tah nodded his head. "You'll find yourself even more consumed with Clara now. She's a part of you. Mating is so much more than marriage is."

"You okay?" Logan asked.

"Tired," Tah admitted. "I wanted to find you. Hope I'm not interrupting anything."

"What's wrong?" Logan asked then grabbed Tah's arm, his eyes huge with panic. "Abby? Did something happen? Did the transfusion not work?"

He felt the tension leave Tah as a genuine smile took over his face. "Abby's fine. She's resting, actually resting. Her cheeks are rosy with color. It was like watching a miracle the way she seemed to revive with my blood. That's why I headed up here to catch you. I was hoping to talk to Clara, to offer her my thanks. I'd like to see if she and I could start fresh and talk."

"Jesus, you scared me for a minute. I'm so glad Abby is doing better." Logan heaved a sigh of relief. "And I'm hoping for a fresh start here for Clara, as well. I'd like for you and Reno to accept her as part of the pride now that we're together."

Tah nodded. "I'll say something to Reno. She's your mate. That makes her family. We still need to talk to her, though. Who knows what else she might be able to tell us?"

"We've talked about that. I'd like to take her to get her stuff. She hid it before she triggered the alarm. She has a phone she can use to contact her Uncle Thomas. She seems to think he'd be the best one to talk to you and fill us all in on everything they know. I think she's a little overwhelmed by all this."

"All this?" Tah questioned.

"Us mating. The pride. You."

"So Reno was right about her deferring to me."

Logan nodded. "I haven't had a chance to discuss it with her, but I can tell she views you with a sort of reverence."

"Do you mind if I speak with her before you leave?" Tah asked. "I'd like to let her know how much what she shared means to me, to us."

Logan felt his cheeks heat. "Let me get her a shirt first. I sort of ripped hers earlier."

Tah threw his head back and laughed. "I've been there. I can go grab something of Abby's if you want. They look like they share a similar build. At least before Abby became pregnant."

"That'd be great."

"I'll bring it up. I'd appreciate it if you'd bring her to the office before you go out. I'd really like the chance to set things right with her."

"No problem," Logan assured him. "Let me just grab a shirt for me and I'll head down with you. Be quicker that way."

"I'll run ahead and grab something and meet you back at the stairs. I don't want to disturb Abby."

"Sounds good," Logan agreed.

He hurried into his room and grabbed a fresh shirt and tugged it over his head. He'd left his socks and shoes in Clara's room so he shoved his feet into a pair of sneakers. He'd get the others when he took her a shirt. He'd have to talk to her about moving into his room. They were mates now. It just made sense. He definitely didn't want to think about not having her in his bed from now on.

Never had sex been like that before. Was that they way it was with mates? More intense? More sensual? Just more on every level? He could easily recall the feel of her flesh against his. Nothing had ever felt so right. He hadn't been lying to her when he said he hadn't been with a woman since he'd left the Marines. It wasn't that they hadn't offered, either. He'd left the bar with a few but had ended up taking them to their homes and leaving them there…alone.

It wasn't even that he hadn't been interested. He had. But there'd been no follow-through. It just hadn't felt right. He'd been teasing when he said maybe he'd been waiting for her, but who knew? Maybe he had. Maybe some part of him had known that there was someone far greater out there that was meant just for him, a love that he needed to be ready for. He'd seen stranger things happen, like finding out your best friends were a lion and tiger. Now he was mated to someone just like them.

Which made him sit down for a minute and catch his breath. He'd mated a shifter, a lioness. Clara would turn into a lioness at some point while he stood watching. What would that be like? To watch his mate become something so different, to be different and yet, still be Clara? He'd always been on the same side of a situation as Reno and Tah. This time he wouldn't be. He'd be the one standing on the porch with their mates watching them run off with his mate. It was a weird concept to wrap his head around.

He was all about being a team player, but what would he do the first time he and Clara faced battle together? He knew it was coming. They all did. It was only a matter of time before another band of hunters came in looking for them. And from what Clara had said, the group Harlan had been with had been nothing compared to what they might face. They were still stretched thin with not enough people around on their side. Could Clara change that with one phone call?

So much to think about and take in. Things were changing so quickly. Every day seemed to bring something more, and rarely were there answers without more questions. Life was interesting, that was for sure. But it was all starting to take a toll, as well. They were essentially flying blind. Tah had been captured. Reno had been captured. They'd been attacked once, and Amia had been tagged by the Blanes. She could have led some of them to Colorado. They wouldn't be able to pinpoint where her signal had disappeared, but they would know to look in Colorado. So it could be just a matter of time before someone stumbled across them.

Chances were, Finn taking the tracker wouldn't matter in the long run. The Blanes would know something was up when they found it abandoned somewhere. It might buy them a little more time, but the cold hard truth was that they needed to be prepared for a major war to happen. They needed weapons and people. People they could trust. What they didn't need was Finn, Murphy and Zane off running around instead of being there where they needed them.

The wolves weren't there anymore, and Logan knew Tah wouldn't call them back unless it was an emergency. They all knew Jess and her mates were dealing with something big of their own. But the pride did need additional people. Shifters preferably. Or at least those with some knowledge of what it was the pride was facing. But it wasn't like they could just take an ad out in the paper.

Help Wanted. Anyone with experience kicking hunter ass. Shifting ability a plus.

That wouldn't go over well. And that left them where they were currently. Overworked and spread far too thin. Three of them had been injured when Harlan Jones had attacked. Tah and Logan had both been shot. Abby had been banged and bruised up. They'd been lucky, very lucky. What happened if luck ran out? What happened if there was an injury Diane and the Professor couldn't take care of? What if one of them died?

He shook those thoughts from his head. They would only serve to drive him crazy. He headed out the door at a jog and turned for the stairs, expecting to find Tah waiting impatiently for him, or at least waiting to give him grief over taking so long. But he wasn't there so Logan went on down to the main floor to see if someone else had caught Tah for something.

"Hey, Logan," Kenzie said. "I figured you'd be in the control room with Reno and Tah."

"What's up?" he asked.

Kenzie looked a little uncomfortable.

"Spill it," he ordered, crossing his arms over his chest.

"Just head to the control room," Kenzie answered quietly. "You'll find out there."

"Fuck!" Logan roared and headed out to see what was going on. If it was more hunters, they were screwed.

Chapter Six

Clara paced the room as she waited for Logan to return. She pulled the phone out from under the mattress and checked the screen to make sure she and Logan hadn't damaged it when they'd been mating on the bed. Remembering that had her grinning like a loon. Then she paced a little more waiting for Logan.

After several more minutes, she was wound tight. It didn't help that the phone was just lying on the bed now, mocking her. She should have given it to Logan before he left, sort of out-of-sight, out-of-mind thing. Now all she could think about was calling. Especially since Logan had pretty much assured her it wouldn't be a problem. He'd offered her his phone, said he'd make sure Tah understood how much it meant to her, and Logan hadn't exactly asked her to wait. Had it been implied, though?

God, she hated this. She wanted to talk to her uncle and tell him all about Logan. She'd found her mate! Logan wouldn't care, would he? He'd understand that she just needed to make the call, particularly if it brought them the help they needed. Logan was her mate. Of course he'd support her. And once the rest of them understood she was calling for help and not to bring more trouble, they'd understand, too. At least, she prayed they would because she knew as she reached for the phone she wasn't going to put it down this time.

It rang three times before anyone answered, and it wasn't the voice she was expecting to hear when someone finally spoke.

"Walker's Trading Post. How can I help you?" Lydia's voice came over the line.

"It's Clara."

"Where the hell have you been? We've been going crazy looking for you. You can't just disappear every time you want."

"Uncle Thomas knew where I was going."

"Oh," Lydia answered, and Clara heard something in her voice.

"What is it? What's going on?"

"Your uncle left just after you did. We haven't heard from him, either. I thought maybe the two of you were together."

"God, I hope he didn't go looking for me in Montana," Clara said. "I really need to talk to him"

"Montana!" Lydia exploded. "I told you to stay away from there. Do you have a death wish?"

"I'm not there anymore. I moved on. And the rise here is glorious when the sky awakens." It was the code they were to use if they ever felt they had information about the one they all searched for, the leader they prayed would come. Tah.

"Where are you, Clara?" Lydia's voice was soft again, quiet and calm. The sudden change was unnerving. "Have you approached anyone?"

Clara felt the hairs on the back of her neck raise. Something was way off with Lydia. She could hear it in the other woman's voice. Lydia was hiding something.

"Who's there with you? Who did Uncle Thomas leave in charge of the store?"

"Me."

Clara knew Lydia was lying then. Uncle Thomas would never leave Lydia in charge. It wasn't just because he didn't really trust Lydia. He wouldn't leave anyone who wasn't a shifter in charge of the store. No exceptions. A shifter in need of help would usually only turn to another shifter for help, not a human.

"Who's there with you?" Clara asked again.

"No one at the moment. Where are you? When can we expect you back? I want to hear more about what you've found."

"I'm not coming back for a while," Clara said carefully.

"What do you mean? I just told you Thomas is missing. We need you back here. I need you back here. We'll discuss what you've found out, find your uncle and figure out where to go from there."

"I've found my mate," Clara admitted, not willing to say anymore about finding Tah. And she really wanted Lydia to be happy for her. Clara needed a mother's understanding right now, and Lydia was the closest thing to a mom she'd ever had. "I'm staying with him and his pride for right now."

"There's a whole pride with him? He's a shifter? Is he where the sky awakens?" Clara didn't answer, and Lydia seemed to grow more agitated. "Where are they located? I'll come to you."

"I found Amia," Clara said softly as disappointment washed through her. No congratulations or I'm so happy for you from Lydia. So she'd fired back, just to see how Lydia would react, to see if the woman's heart had softened at all when it came to her blood daughter.

"I told you to leave her alone!" Lydia cried out over the phone. "If you mated someone connected to her, you might as well have signed your death certificate. She'll get you killed, Clara. I've warned you to let it be. You can't save her."

"Why? Why can't Amia be good? What if she's like you, Lydia? What if she defied the Blanes, as well?" It was an old argument, but Clara always expected a new answer from Lydia. She was always disappointed.

"Please, that girl is a Blane by blood. I married into that tribe of monsters. It's different. Blood will always tell. She's been a curse since she was born. I tried to keep her safe, keep her quiet, and look where that led. Your father dead and me running for my life." Harsh words that Lydia hadn't always uttered—not in the very beginning.

"None of that was her fault," Clara reminded her. "She's just as innocent in all of this as you were. You're wrong about her. You've always been wrong about her. Open your eyes, Lydia. I told you, she saved my life. I owe her."

"You owe her nothing. If you'd brought her back here like you wanted to, we'd probably all be dead."

"Who else is there? Is Gideon there?"

Gideon had grown up with her dad and Uncle Thomas. He was the one normally in charge when her uncle left.

"Gideon took Ariel and Griffin to look for Thomas. I need you home now. I don't care what you have going on. We need you here."

"I've mated. You know what that means."

"I don't care," Lydia screeched. "You're my family. I need you. You have to come back from Colorado, now."

Clara stilled and glanced at the phone. "How do you know where I am?"

"Just a guess," Lydia said, her voice filled with quiet calm once more. "Come home to me," she crooned.

"You're tracing the call, aren't you?" Clara asked, a little shocked that Lydia would do such a thing.

"Come home, Clara."

"I am home," Clara whispered and disconnected the call, cutting off whatever Lydia had been screaming on the other end.

Nothing made sense. Uncle Thomas was gone and hadn't checked in? It seemed logical that Gideon would go after her uncle if he'd been gone too long. But Gideon wouldn't have taken anyone with him. He was very much a lone shifter. He skirted the edges of their makeshift pride, never fully joining. So why would he take Ariel and Griffin with him? Ariel especially. Gideon was all about protecting the females of the pride. He wouldn't take Ariel with him...unless he thought there was danger.

Dread filled her. Where was Logan? She really needed Logan right now. God, she needed to leave. She needed to go find her Uncle Thomas or even Gideon at this point. She just needed to find out what the hell was going on. She tried the door and found it unlocked this time. Did Logan leave it that way on purpose? Was he waiting for her to join him in his room? What was she supposed to do? God, she couldn't focus.

She shook from the surge of adrenaline coursing through her. There was no way she was going to be able to stay cooped up. She grabbed her ripped shirt from the door and pulled it on backwards so it was opened in the back. She took a deep breath and pushed open the door, then took a tentative step into the hall. When no alarms went off and no one stepped out to stop her, she ventured farther, going to the room she knew was Logan's. The door was open, but he wasn't inside. She glanced toward the stairs she knew led to the main level. Where the fuck was her mate? Their connection wasn't completely formed yet. It would take a little bit longer before she'd be able to sense him and locate him by those feelings. She'd just have to grab one of his shirts and see if she could find him.

Logan found Reno, Amia, Vic and Tah crowded in the control room. There was no mistaking Clara's voice as she spoke to someone on the phone. But what phone? He hadn't taken her his phone yet. Then it clicked in his head. Clara had told him Amia had left her phone in the room when she'd gone up to talk to Clara.

"You set her up," he accused Amia, but her face was chalk white and she wasn't paying attention to him, so he turned to Tah. "What the fuck, man? This is the way we treat mates now?"

"You've mated with her then?" Reno asked, though Logan could see he was keeping an eye on Amia.

"Yes," Logan said. "She asked if she could make a phone call, even admitted Amia had left her phone behind. I didn't think it would be an issue." Okay, so he hadn't known she was going to make the call while he was gone. But he trusted her. She'd felt the need to call her uncle now instead of waiting. But that was a woman's voice on the phone talking to Clara.

"Who is that?" Logan asked.

"My mother," Amia whispered so low Logan had to strain to hear. "She's talking to my mother." And just like that Amia went down.

Reno roared and shoved his way to her, sweeping her up from the floor where she'd crumpled and curling her against his chest. He turned to glare at Logan before turning to Tah.

"We'll talk later." With that he whisked Amia away.

"Amia's mom is alive?" Logan asked.

Tah stared hard at him. "It's your mate talking to her. Shit, we knew Clara was keeping something from us, but this? She should have told Amia."

"And when did you give her a chance? Any of you? When you were roaring at her in that meeting you held? The one where everyone in the goddamn room was sided against her? When you had her locked in a room for a week? You went to talk to her then, didn't you? Gave her a chance to talk? No, that's right. You didn't give a fuck about her. So when was she supposed to tell any of you a damn thing?"

"Stand down, Logan. Amia's reeling to the point she just passed the fuck out. I'm sure hearing her mother's voice was the last thing she expected when she left that phone for Clara. Amia's upset right now which means Reno's upset, as well. What a fucking mess!"

The conversation began playing again, and Logan realized they'd recorded it. He might not have soaked in all that was said, but he had heard one thing loud and clear. She'd told the woman she was talking to, Amia's mom, that she was home. She'd found her mate, and she was home. That was all he cared about at the moment. He turned angry eyes back on Tah.

"Then I guess Amia shouldn't have pretended to be friendly with Clara only to set her up. Clara gave you the information you needed to help Abby and probably saved your mate's life. And this is how you all repay her."

"Logan—"

"No." Logan cut Tah off, slashing his hand through the air. "Amia's upset which means Reno's upset? Really? Are those the words you just uttered to me? Well, guess what? I've been trying to convince my mate that she has nothing to worry about now that we're mated, that you'll all accept her the way I do. I told her you'd give her a chance and be okay with her calling her pride. Guess I was fucking wrong on both accounts. How about this? My mate is uncertain, and now, I am, too." Logan shook his head in disgust. "I never thought we'd be the type of pride that gave one mate preference over another. And I never anticipated feeling second best to Reno."

"Logan…" Tah started again but trailed off as Logan just shook his head again.

"Your words said it all." Logan looked toward the door and found Clara standing there. He wasn't sure how much she'd heard, but her eyes said she'd caught the gist of it. He turned and walked to Clara, taking her hand and linking their fingers. "I'm taking Clara to find her things. We'll be back later."

"Logan, don't," Tah said. It wasn't an order. It was a plea from a friend, from someone Logan thought of as a brother, which meant the pain Logan was feeling was raw and cut deep.

"Reno's upset," Logan said. "You'd better go check on him."

He tugged Clara with him from the room and headed down the hall toward the front door. He needed air.

"Logan." Clara whispered his name as they walked away from the house toward the woods.

"It's okay."

"No, it's not. I can feel your pain. Your heart is crying." She stepped in front of him, blocking his path and forcing him to look at her.

He gritted his teeth against the surge of anger he felt when he saw the tears streaming down her cheeks. Once again, his mate was in tears. It tore him up to see her this way.

"I didn't mean to hurt you, Logan. If I'd know this would happen, I'd…"

"You'd what? You'd have continued to try and deny me as your mate?"

She nodded her head slowly. "I'm tearing you apart."

Funny how she echoed exactly what he was feeling. Only it wasn't her actions tearing him apart, but the wash of emotion staining her cheeks.

"No, you're not," he said, pulling her into his arms and holding her tight against him. "None of this is on you. Tah said what he said. Only he can own the words he spoke. That's on no one else."

"Finding your mate is supposed to be a joyous occasion, a celebration."

"It can be. It will be. I promise, Clara. We'll be okay."

"I'm not sure of that," she countered.

"What's wrong?" he asked, suddenly realizing what he was feeling wasn't all him. Some of it was her feelings bleeding into him.

"Something's wrong, Logan. My Uncle Thomas is missing. Lydia said he left her in charge, but it doesn't feel right. He'd never leave her in charge."

"Your uncle doesn't trust her?"

Clara shook her head.

"Why would he keep her around then?"

"Because my dad sent her to us. He wouldn't have done that for just anyone."

"I can't wrap my head around all this. Amia's mom has been with you?"

"It's a long story, and I'd rather tell it once. I get the feeling my phone call has earned me another inquisition."

"I'll be right beside you the whole time. I'll say it as many times as it takes to sink in. You will never stand alone again."

"I don't want to tear you apart. That's not what mates do."

"And I've already told you. None of this is your fault. Whatever choices Tah makes, we'll face it together."

"I think I'm going to love you," Clara whispered.

"I think we're going to love each other," Logan answered and bent to brush his lips over hers.

It was an odd thing to have his heart so filled with love for a woman while at the same time being ripped apart over what was happening with his two best friends. God help them, they needed to be sticking together, not doing this. He gripped Clara's fingers and started walking again. He really hoped this new beginning didn't portend of another relationship ending.

* * * *

"We should call for help," Zane said again as he and Murphy sat in the Jeep. "We have no idea who has Finn or why. We could be walking into a trap. And what then?"

"That's why I'm going in after him alone when we do find him," Murphy said.

"The hell you are," Zane grunted, glaring at Murphy in challenge. "How the fuck do you plan to stop me from going with you?"

"I don't want to fight you, Zane."

Zane laughed. "Good thing. I'm fully in touch with my panther. I can summon his strength in this form, as well. You wouldn't stand a chance against me."

Murphy just looked at him, and once again Zane wondered what the other man held inside him. Something was blocking Zane from being able to scent it or pick up on any trait signs of it. Murphy was either very good, or someone or something was protecting him. What? Or who?

"Tell me about your family," Zane said. "You said Finn left with you when you were forced to go."

Murphy sighed, scrubbed a hand over his face, leaned his head back and closed his eyes. Zane could see he was bone-weary but wasn't sure if it was from their lack of rest or Murphy's connection with Finn. Whoever had Finn must have tortured him most of the night. Murphy had been a mess of pain, yet somehow managed to keep his focus on finding his brother. Unfortunately, they had little idea of where to search now, just the feelings that Murphy was getting from Finn. Whoever had him was good at covering their trail.

"My dad," Murphy finally said. "It near broke him when he came home and found mum. He blamed me and rightly so. If she'd no been protecting me, she'd still be alive."

"You don't know that," Zane countered, letting his anger show through. "People die."

"They were there looking for me," Murphy explained. "I musta been careless and let m'self be seen at some point."

"Or someone else blabbed about what you were," Zane suggested.

Murphy shook his head. "No. I can't believe anyone would do that."

"You'd be surprised what people will do for the right amount."

"We left our dad, two brothers, and...and a sister behind. I can't believe any one of them would want that to happen. Our mum died!" Murphy rubbed his chest again as he spoke.

"Still hurting?" Zane asked.

"Just an ache. They must be giving him a break this morning. I feel more of a numbness filtering through me now than any kind of pain."

"Numbness?" Zane asked and felt a chill of foreboding go through him. "Fuck, Murphy, that's not good. We need to find him now. Right the fuck now."

Chapter Seven

It was late when Logan headed them back toward the house. They'd spent a lot of time just walking around in companionable silence. They both had a lot on their minds. There was a big part of Clara that wanted to leave and go in search of her uncle, but she couldn't. She would never leave Logan. And right now, with the amount of pain he had radiating from him, she was deeply concerned.

No one was around when they walked in, and she thought they'd make it back upstairs without Logan seeing anyone. But luck wasn't with them. Tah's voice stopped them at the bottom of the stairs.

"Logan," Tah called.

Clara felt her mate blow out a breath of air. His shoulders tensed, and he dropped his head forward for a minute.

"We need to talk," Tah said.

"Is Amia all right?" Logan asked without lifting his head.

"She's resting," Tah answered.

"Good." Logan tugged Clara and went up another step.

"Logan, we need to talk about this."

Clara looked back, taking in the pain her alpha was feeling. It was as intense as that of her mate.

"Later, Tah. I'm tired, and I just don't feel like getting into all this right now." He eased an arm behind Clara and urged her up the stairs in front of him. "By the way," he called over his shoulder.

"Clara's moving into my room. We'll be down when we wake up in the morning. I showed her around tonight, walked the perimeter. She can work with me for the next few days until we figure things out."

"There's nothing to figure out," Tah swore.

"In the morning, Tah," Logan reminded him. "Go be with your mate and let me be with mine."

With that, Logan propelled them both up the stairs and down the hall to his room. The door was still open and someone had moved the things from the room she'd been in before to his. She tossed her pack on the floor while Logan closed the door behind them and heaved a sigh. She turned and saw him undressing.

"He's hurting, too," she told her mate.

"I don't give a shit."

"Yes, you do. That's why you're so upset."

"Let's just go to sleep. We'll deal with whatever we need to in the morning."

"I'm so sorry," she whispered.

"You have no reason to be sorry," he said, just as he did every time she apologized. "Come on. Let's take a shower."

She followed him into the bathroom, stripping while he played with the water until he got it to whatever temperature he'd decided on. His eyes devoured her when he turned and found her naked.

"You are the most beautiful woman I've ever seen."

"I don't deserve you," she whispered.

He smiled and made quick work of shedding the rest of his clothes. He slid the glass door open and held a hand out to her. "Why don't you step inside and let me show you how much you do deserve me?"

She shivered with anticipation, her nipples pebbling into hard buds and sending a streak of hot need down through her core. She took his hand and stepped in, moving under the hot spray to make room for the even hotter man at her back. He wound his hands around her waist and tugged her back against his broad chest. She turned her head to glance back at him then moaned as his teeth grazed her neck.

"I need you," he murmured.

"Yes." She needed him, too, desperately. She turned in his arms until she faced him. "Right here," she urged. "Take me."

He took her mouth as he reached down to cup her ass and lift her. She prayed his feet would stay firm on the mesh matt in the bottom of the shower. Her back brushed the wall and she lifted her legs to wrap around his waist. He used his hold on her ass to position her over his cock then let gravity take over as she slid down on him. Sheer pleasure.

"Take me," she dared. "Take me just the way you want to."

He shook his head. "Not here."

"Then sate the need enough so we can clean up and move this elsewhere."

He grunted in agreement and began fucking into her slow and easy. The angle had every stroke striking deep. She clutched his shoulders and held on as he rode her. There wasn't much she could do in this position, not without putting them at risk of losing their balance and falling. So she just held tight and let him control the loving.

She eased her hand down between their bodies and rubbed over her clit.

"That's right, baby. Come all over my dick. Let me feel that pussy milking my cum out."

"Yes! Oh, God! Yes!"

She bucked against him as her orgasm hit, arching so that the only things touching the wall were her ass and the top of her head. Logan dropped his chin to her chest and found a puckered nipple with his mouth. She cried out again as he pulled it deep before nipping it with his teeth. He moved to the other one and treated it the same.

"Logan." She wailed his name as another orgasm hit.

Before she realized his intent, he pulled out and dropped to his knees in the tub. She balanced on shaky feet, leaning against the wall to help steady herself. One of his arms pinned her belly to the wall while he used the fingers of the other hand to spread her flushed cunt wide for his perusal. He took her up again with his mouth, licking and sucking on her pussy, lapping the juices spilling out of her as if it were the tastiest treat he'd ever devoured.

Clara had one hand braced by her hip on the wall and the other wrapped in his hair, holding his head exactly where she wanted it.

He eased off her clit and nipped her inner thigh.

"Look at me," he ordered then smiled as their gazes clashed. "Feeling a little on edge, baby? A little primal?"

"What?" She struggled to emerge from the cocoon of pleasure.

"Your eyes are glowing the most beautiful shade of yellow," he murmured huskily against her skin.

He placed another stinging kiss against her inner thigh and stood up. "Let's get washed and move this to the bedroom."

"You didn't come," she said. "Let me catch my breath, and I'll take care of that for you." She reached out and wrapped her fingers around his cock, giving it a squeeze.

Logan groaned with pleasure but took her hand and moved it away. "I want you on your knees, baby. But it's not your mouth I want to fuck." He kissed her hard and fast then turned her around so the water poured over her again. "I'm feeling a bit primal myself," he said over her shoulder. "Think you could handle things a little rough?"

She felt a shiver of anticipation go through her. She glanced back, letting him see the excitement she felt. "I can handle it as rough as you want to give it."

He slapped her ass with the palm of his hand, and she knew from the burn his handprint would remain on her skin. "Wash quick."

She sped through, making quick work and moving behind him to wash her hair while he soaped up and rinsed. They swapped spots so she could rinse then switched again. He gave her another swat when he stepped out, leaving her alone to quickly rinse the conditioner out of her hair. Could she unleash with him? He was human after all, even though he was her mate. It wasn't exactly a question she'd ever asked another shifter.

She turned off the water and opened the door. He was already gone, so she grabbed a towel and dried as best she could. She toweled her hair, leaving it in a wild mane around her. It was still wet, but she had other priorities at the moment. Logan, and seeing what he had in store for her.

She found him in the bedroom with a pair of cuffs dangling from his fingers. Her gaze wanted to remain between his thighs where his cock bobbed and teased her. Instead, she bounced it between his erection and what he held.

"Cuffs?" she questioned, licking her lips and forcing her gaze back up to his.

"I'd hate for my kitty to go crazy with her claws," he purred. "Unless...you're afraid."

She narrowed her eyes at him. "Cuffs? I'd say you're the one who's afraid. What's the matter, Logan? Can't handle a shifter for a mate?"

Logan grinned. "Maybe I just like my sex with a little more flavor to it."

It was a challenge, and she knew it. But his pain wasn't present at the moment, and she'd do anything to keep it that way. She walked over to him and held her wrists out. Even be cuffed.

"On the bed," he ordered.

She moved easily to comply, crawling up toward the headboard on her hands and knees.

"Perfect," he crooned behind her. He ran his hands over her ass, smoothing and rubbing the round curves, and she closed her eyes, just waiting for another sharp slap. He didn't give one, though. Instead, he whispered in her ear. "Hold real still for me."

He snapped one cuff on, and she blinked her eyes open to see he'd attached the cuffs to some type of chain that was wrapped around the thick post of wood that decorated the middle of the headboard. He took her other wrist and wrapped the second cuff around it while she watched. The heat in his eyes, the lust and need, had her body on fire with a fresh dose of carnal desire.

"I'm going to fuck you, Clara."

"God, yes."

"I'm going to fuck your sweet pussy until you scream my name." He trailed his fingers over her shoulder and down along her side until he reached her hip. He opened his palm and ran it over her ass cheek. "I love your ass. So round and perfect." His gaze flicked up to hers. "I want to fuck you there, fuck that sweet, tight ass of yours."

She gulped as her pussy grew damper and her ass clenched with hot need. "Yes," she whispered. She wanted him there, every inch of him.

"You'll take me there?" he asked.

She nodded. "Anywhere and everywhere," she promised. "Anywhere and everywhere."

He shifted onto the bed behind her, two big fingers spearing her pussy from behind while he cupped her hip with the other hand. "So wet. So ready for whatever I want."

"Yes," she agreed, desperate to feel him bury his cock deep inside her again.

He pulled his fingers out and she glanced back just in time to see him suck them into his mouth.

"Mhmm," he said as he licked and sucked her juices off them. "You have the sweetest tasting pussy. I could gorge myself on your delicious cunt every day and still not get enough."

"Logan." She moaned his name.

"Shhh." He growled against her flesh. "Soon, baby. Soon."

He leaned forward and ran his lips over the top curve of her ass. His hands massaged and separated the globes while he continued to place kisses over her skin. She was shaking with arousal. At this point, she'd come as soon as he thrust his dick inside. He trailed his lips up her spine, using his hands to press her down until she lay flat on her stomach on the bed. He nipped at her shoulder then moved up her neck to her ear.

"When I'm done, when I've sated us both, I'll take the cuffs off," he promised. "And if you're a really good girl…" He sucked her earlobe between his teeth and flicked it with his tongue. "I'll let you cuff me next time."

"Fuck!" she exclaimed as visions filled her head. "Fuck me! Now!"

His chuckle washed over her skin as he used his knees to spread her legs wider. His body pinned hers to the bed as he fucked his cock between the seam of her sex and the bed. "Rough and dirty, baby. Can you handle that?" he asked again.

She knew he wouldn't take her that way if she said no. He'd stop and give her what she could handle. But they were connected now as only mates could be, and his need was hers. She wanted him rough. She wanted him hard. Craved a darker side of loving.

"Stop talking and fuck my pussy," she ordered.

With another grunt, he reached down and pressed his cock into her. Firm hands gripped her hips, and Logan slammed deep. She was so wet and beyond ready for him. Every stroke was welcomed by her slick walls. Every penetration was met with her pressing into him, wanting it even deeper. Her clit rubbed along the bedding, the friction giving just the right amount of additional pressure to send her screaming into orgasm.

He slammed harder, rode her faster, taking her orgasm and dragging it out with every touch of skin-on-skin. He reached up and spread his hand at the base of her neck, thumb on one side, fingers on the other. She lifted her knees just a bit, switching the angle on him and cried out as he rewarded her with a deliciously deep thrust.

Her hands were fisted in the bedding where the cuffs kept them. She wanted to reach for him, to grip his thighs with her nails. She wanted to scratch and claw, to bite. Maybe it was a good thing he'd cuffed her. The more dominant he became, the more turned on she got.

"Come for me again," he ordered. "I want my cock dripping with your juices when I work it up your ass."

"Ahhh." She sighed as she jerked beneath him with another orgasm. Just the thought of him working his thick cock up her ass was enough to have her awash in more pleasure.

He pulled his shaft free and moved off the bed toward a bag she'd been too distracted to notice earlier. He rummaged around, obviously looking for something, then pulled out a bottle of what looked like oil. She wondered what other toys he might be hiding in there. He turned to her, twisting the cap off and dropping it beside her on the bed.

"Going to get you nice and slick for me."

"Yes," she agreed. "Don't tease me."

"Oh, baby, I plan to do nothing but please you."

Slick fingers slid between her cheeks and skimmed over her anus. He rubbed the oil in and kept rubbing until he finally pressed the tip of his thumb inside. He used the other hand to drizzle oil onto her crack and worked more of it into her until he was pumping two fingers in and out of her backdoor.

"Oh, God! Logan! Fuck me! Please! Fuck me!" She was on fire, beyond ready for anal play.

Finally, his fingers disappeared. She heard him recapping the oil then felt the nudge of his cock at her anus. He pulled back and ran his cock along the seam, easily sliding through the oil remaining there. His hands stroked and massaged her cheeks, spreading them, and she imagined him watching his dick glide against her there.

"Ready?" he asked, his voice so husky and deep it was almost guttural.

"Yes."

With a groan, he lodged the tip against her anus again. This time he pressed in until the crown filled her ass. He kept pressing, pushing through the tight ring of muscle and not stopping until she felt the weight of his balls against her. She dropped her head to the bed and breathed through her nose. So good. It was so good, too fucking good. She wouldn't last.

"Not going to last." Logan grunted, mirroring her exact thoughts.

"Then fuck me. Fuck me hard," she commanded.

She muffled her screams of pleasure in the bedding as he went about following her order. He slammed into her again and again, until they were nothing more than a blur of motion and shared ecstasy. She heard a loud snap and only realized it was the cuffs breaking when she no longer had to wish for the ability to reach back and touch him. Instead, her nails were sinking into the backs of his thighs, urging him even faster.

"Ahh, fuck!" Logan yelled. "I'm coming, baby. I'm coming."

She cried out as another orgasm rocked through her. He pressed his cock impossibly deeper and held it there while he filled her ass with his cum.

"Mine," he whispered at her ear. "Every inch of you belongs to me."

He might not be a shifter, but he was pure alpha male. He was perfectly matched to her.

"Mine," she declared, turning her head and gripping his jaw with her teeth. "You are mine and mine alone. I'll kill anyone who tries to take you from me."

He moved his head, sliding from her grip easily and kissing her softly on the lips. "We belong, Clara. With each other."

She nodded her head.

He eased out of her and collapsed on the bed beside her. He lifted one of her hands where the cuff was still attached and chuckled softly. "I guess you won't be using these on me."

"We'll buy a new pair," she vowed and dozed off with his warm laughter in her ear.

Chapter Eight

The house was quiet as Logan led Clara down the stairs early the next morning. He could feel the tremble she tried to hide and felt an answering anger inside him. This was his home, his family, damn it! His mate should never have to feel unwelcomed, or worse, unwanted here. He heard voices coming from the office and tugged Clara with him.

"I'm with you," he reminded her softly just outside the door.

She nodded, but he could see the unease, the uncertainty in her eyes. He pushed open the door and stepped in with his arm wrapped around Clara. He knew his stance was aggressive and didn't give a fuck. His gaze swept the room. Tah and Abby were there along with Diane and the Professor. No Reno. No Amia.

"If anyone has anything to say, you can say it now." He grunted.

Abby turned her head and zeroed in on them. Christ the changes in her! It was like seeing the Abby who'd walked into the bar so long ago, only pregnant. She looked healthy and so happy, her grin was practically lighting up the room. She charged across the room toward them and wrapped Clara up in a hug.

"Thank you," she said over and over again. "You saved my life. I know you did so don't shake your head at me," she admonished when Clara started doing just that. "You did, and everyone in this room knows it."

She released Clara only to wrap Logan up in her embrace. "Logan. You've mated. A lioness, no less. I'm so happy for you two."

She tugged both their hands and backed toward the couch. "Come. Sit down. I have a million questions."

"Good to see you're feeling better," Logan said and meant it. This wasn't the greeting he'd been bracing for.

An arm snaked around Abby's waist and Logan watched Tah pull his mate against him. "I'm glad you're feeling better, but you still need to take it easy."

"Hell, no. I feel like I can do anything. If I'd known getting a dose of your blood would be like this, I might have become a vampire."

Tah chuckled.

"One vampire is enough," Logan whispered.

"I heard that, young man," the Professor said. "And you're right. When we're finished up here, I'll want both you and your mate in the lab for some tests. I'll need blood and some of your saliva." He nodded his head toward Clara on the last remark.

"Fuck," Logan muttered under his breath.

"I heard that, too," the Professor informed him. "Ears like a bat," he said when Logan lifted a brow at him.

Diane snorted as she tried to hide a laugh at the Professor's play on Logan's nickname for him.

"I'm Diane," she said, taking Clara's hand. "I can't tell you how lucky we are that you arrived when you did. You really did save Abby. I'd love to talk to you. See what else you might know that could help us out. I'm floundering my way through all this. It would be nice to feel like I was ahead for a change."

"Diane is a genius," Abby countered. "She doesn't flounder through anything."

"I'm sorry," Clara spoke up. "I didn't think about you not knowing what to do during a pregnancy. I just didn't think."

"No reason to be sorry," Diane assured her. "You told us when you did realize, and that's all that matters."

"We're going to have to talk about this need of yours to apologize for everything," Logan said.

"I'm guessing that there are a lot of things you've learned that we could really use," Diane said.

Clara nodded. "I take it Orsai hasn't found you yet then?"

"Who's Orsai?" Tah asked.

"A panther shifter. I just assumed..." She waved it off. "Never mind. He's been a fountain of wisdom for us, and I imagine for other shifters he's happened upon, as well. He knows more than anyone I've ever met."

"How can we get in touch with him?" Tah asked.

Clara shrugged. "You don't get in touch with him. He gets in touch with you."

"I guess we'll just have to wait then," Tah said with a sigh.

"I'm going to apologize one more time," Clara said and Logan sent her a fierce look, which she ignored as she faced Abby. "I shouldn't have said what I did to you. It was wrong, and—"

"No, it wasn't," Abby interrupted. "Amia told me what you saw when you were just a child. It scares me." She placed both hands on her burgeoning belly. "That our son might see similar things some day."

"Never," Tah swore, and Logan seconded him.

"We won't let anything happen to you or your son," Logan vowed. He pulled Clara close to him. He'd never been one for ignoring the elephant in the room. "How is Amia today? I know yesterday was a shock."

"I'd say," Abby said, sitting and patting the couch next to her.

Clara looked at Logan as if to see what he thought. It brought home once more just how unsure she was. He shrugged, leaving it up to her as to what she did. She eased away from him and sat gingerly beside Abby on the sofa.

"Tah told me all about it. Amia's mom, alive and living with you and your uncle this whole time."

"I wanted to tell her," Clara admitted.

"I'm gathering you weren't allowed to," Abby said and Clara nodded.

Logan felt his heart swell with tenderness when Abby took both of Clara's hands in hers and squeezed.

"It's not your fault any more than anything has been Amia's. You both have been little more than pawns in a game neither of you realized you were even playing."

"Still, I don't want to be the cause of any trouble for anyone." She glanced at Logan as if he hadn't known exactly what she was referring to.

"Nonsense," Abby admonished. "If you're talking about Tah, Reno and Logan, they'll work it out."

Logan almost felt sorry for Tah when Abby sent a pointed look his way. Tah just sighed and rubbed a hand over the back of his neck.

"Won't you?" The point was loud and clear to everyone in the room. They'd work it out or else.

Logan did chuckle then.

"The same goes for you, Logan," Abby stated, cutting his chuckle off. "You will work it out."

Tah was the one who snickered now.

"We are a family," Abby said loudly, and Logan figured it was for all their benefit. "Families squabble, but they make up."

"I hope so," Clara said.

"This Lydia, Amia's mother," Tah said. "You think she might have been tracking the call?"

Clara nodded. "I… She knew where I was. She told me to come home from Colorado. I didn't tell anyone but my uncle where I was headed, and he didn't know I was following Amia here."

"So your uncle knew you were following Amia?" Tah questioned.

Logan moved to stand behind where Clara sat on the couch. He leaned his hip against the back and laid a hand on his mate's shoulder. She would face nothing alone ever again.

"Yes. He was the one who encouraged it after I found her the first time, and she rescued me."

"Then why wouldn't he want you to bring Amia back with you?" Abby asked.

"He was afraid for her."

"But he could have protected her from the Blanes. They might have never gotten their hands on her," Diane countered.

"It wasn't the Blanes he was worried about, or at least not the ones you're referring to."

"Lydia?" Abby asked.

Clara nodded. "He was afraid of what Lydia might do. My uncle travels, and he wouldn't have been able to take Amia and me with him all the time. There would have been times when Lydia could have gotten to her."

"Why would Lydia harm her own daughter?" Tah questioned.

Clara shrugged. "I don't know. She was broken when she arrived. We didn't even know she had a daughter. She told us her family was gone. She…she tried to rescue my dad from the Blanes but wasn't able to. He died."

"I'm so sorry, Clara," Abby said.

Logan squeezed her shoulder, offering comfort and support.

"He sent Lydia to us. I thought he must have seen something good in her. Uncle Thomas thought the same. When she first arrived, we'd find her crying. She'd wake from nightmares, screaming Amia's name. It's how I learned Amia even existed. It's how Lydia finally confessed who she was. But as the years passed, Lydia became withdrawn and angry. She hated hunters, especially the Blanes. She wasn't the same woman who first came to us by the time I found Amia when we were sixteen," Clara told them. "I guess I've known for a long time that Lydia was bitter. Uncle Thomas said he was watching her. She's all about vengeance, trying to convince some of the younger shifters to attack first, to capture the hunters and subject them to the same treatment."

Logan met Tah's eyes and wondered if Tah was thinking the same thing he was. When Reno had been sent to get information about the Blanes, they'd planned for the possibility of him capturing one and bringing them back. Hell, Amia had even been thrown into one of the small storage rooms downstairs. Would they have tortured her if she hadn't been Reno's mate? Would they have tortured a man if that had been who Reno had brought back with him?

"I can't say I haven't had similar thoughts myself," Abby admitted.

Logan had to agree he had, as well. Hell, after what they'd been through with Harlan Jones, they all would have jumped at the opportunity for a little payback.

"I'm betting it's not the same as Lydia. Her rationality is skewed," Clara said. "If she had her way, she'd hunt down every Blane and kill them. Man, woman, child, infant. It doesn't matter to her. How is that right? How is that just? How many like Amia would have been killed at Lydia's word? I can't believe that the only way to defeat the beast is to become the beast. I have to hold onto the belief there's a better way. There has to be."

"Maybe there's not," Amia said from the doorway. She and Reno stepped into the room. "Maybe death is the only answer."

"No." Clara shook her head, and Logan knew what she was going to do before she rose from the couch. "I'm so sorry, Amia."

"You knew my mother was alive. All this time." There was a world of hurt on Amia's face, and anger—a lot of anger. "You should have told me as soon as Reno confronted you and brought you here," Amia said.

"I wanted to, but there was never the right time to."

"Then you make a right time," Amia gritted out, her voice hard. "You should have found the time to tell me."

"I should have," Clara whispered, and Logan felt his mate hurting for Amia when all Amia seemed focused on was anger.

"When?" Logan challenged. He'd be damned if he sat back and let them railroad Clara into feeling as if she was the bad guy in all this. "When we all stood against her in that room? Or when you went to her room to pretend to be her friend and instead set her up?"

Reno growled, but Logan didn't care.

"Not to mention the fact that maybe, just maybe, this wasn't her secret to tell. Still, what you did… You shouldn't ask for information you're not ready to handle," he said to Amia then looked straight at Reno. "And you should never pretend a friendship just to get what you want."

"Logan." Clara turned to glance back at him.

"It's not okay," he said before she could say anything else. "I don't care what reason they had. It's not okay to treat people this way. And it's got to stop."

"You're right," Amia said. "We should be straight up and honest. Tell people how we feel. Hold nothing back." Each sentence was filled with more anger, as if she was spiraling and couldn't control it.

Logan didn't like the look in Amia's eyes as she spoke. He moved around the couch and headed toward Clara. He didn't get there in time, and Clara did nothing to defend herself. Amia swung her fist and hit Clara on the cheekbone. He heard his mate give a cry of surprise then she was falling back. He caught her and swung her behind him to face Amia.

"What the fuck?" he yelled.

Reno stepped in front of Amia and bared his teeth at Logan.

"Bring it on," Logan challenged. "At least I'm watching and will see it coming."

"Back down, pup," Reno uttered.

"I'm not your fucking pup, pussy."

"Enough," Tah roared, but it was Abby and the Professor who stepped forward.

"That's enough," Abby said quietly. "Diane, check Clara's cheek. Amia, in that chair." She pointed to where she expected Amia to go. "Not a word," she ordered Logan and Reno. "I'm ashamed of you, all of you."

Logan felt like a kid getting chastised.

"I want the three of you out of this office. Now."

"Abby." Tah stepped forward, but his mate was having none of it.

"You take them and get this worked out before something else like this happens."

Logan moved to squat in front of Clara. Her cheek was going to bruise, and he felt the anger building in him.

"I'm fine, Logan," Clara said, and it pissed him off to know she felt as if she'd deserved Amia's punch.

He brushed his knuckles softly over her check, just under the already forming bruise. "I'll get you some ice."

"I've got it," the Professor said, sounding angrier than Logan had ever seen him. The little man was practically vibrating with it. He paused to whisper something to Abby and squeezed her hand, then slammed out of the room.

"I've never been so upset in my life. What is wrong with you guys? We're a family. Family, damn it!" Abby yelled.

She looked as if she might burst into tears. He hated to see Abby upset. They all did. Tah was the Alpha of their pride, but Abby was the heart.

"Why don't I take Amia back to our room for a bit," Reno suggested.

Logan understood what he was trying to do—ease the tension by removing Amia. But it was too late for that. Abby was livid and turned all her anger onto Reno as soon as the words were out of his mouth. Logan shook his head and couldn't help feeling a little sorry for Reno. Even Tah stepped back and looked at Reno with incredulity. Abby vibrated with fury. She stepped right up to Reno and glared up at him.

"Are you challenging me?" she demanded, hands on hips, looking as if she might start breathing fire any minute.

Damn! Logan had never seen Abby like this.

"I said I wanted the three of you out of here. Now. You need to fix whatever is going on. Work. It. Out. Now."

"I need to check on my mate," Reno grumbled, but Logan saw him cast a glance at Tah.

"You're mate is fine. Probably nursing some bruised knuckles to go with her bruised heart." Abby turned to face where Clara and Amia were sitting slightly apart from one another. "Amia, Clara and I are going to sit down and chat, and no one, and I do mean no one, will leave this fucking room until we have it hashed out and settled. Do I make myself fucking clear?" She was all but roaring at the end.

Reno gave a sharp nod. Logan almost laughed as he watched the big tiger shifter skirt around Abby to go squat in front of Amia. He spoke softly to her and kissed her tenderly before standing once again.

Abby turned all her fury onto Tah then, and man was she a sight to behold now. "I don't know what the hell is going on here, but I will not have this in our home. Our home, Tah. Mates coming to blows. Reno and Logan almost following suit. You will fix this, or so help me I don't know what I'll do. We need each other. This isn't a game we're playing. Lives are on the line here. All three of you have almost died. We've killed people and buried them in the fucking woods! We will not start turning on each other!"

She was right. Abby was absolutely right, and Logan felt all his anger fade away.

"You better go," Clara whispered to Logan. "She looks pretty pissed."

"Are you sure you'll be okay?" he asked.

"I don't think Amia meant to hit me," Clara said. "She's hurt. She just needed someone to strike out at. I'm the perfect target."

"That doesn't make it okay," Logan uttered, but he wasn't angry anymore.

He couldn't help the grin that tugged at his lips. For the first time since he'd walked into the control room last night, he felt as if it might be all right.

"We'll fix this," he promised. "This is home. This is where we belong."

"Anywhere you are is home to me," she whispered. "I'm falling in love with you."

"Me, too," he whispered back.

"Logan!" Abby yelled.

Logan shared one last smile with his mate and winked at her before standing and turning to Abby. "Yes, ma'am. I'm leaving." No way was he going to have Abby ask him if he was challenging her.

She stopped him on his way past her and grabbed his hand. "He loves you, Logan."

"I love him, too," Logan assured her.

It didn't matter if she was referring to Tah or Reno. It applied to both of them. They were best friends, brothers. Somehow in all the chaos of what they'd been through, they'd lost sight of that. They'd gotten so wrapped up in doing everything they could to make sure they were secure and protected, that they forgot some other important things. It was time to start remembering.

He glanced up and saw Tah and Reno heading out the front door and moved to join them. The Professor rounded the corner and Logan paused for a minute. The little man looked angry as hell, which was something Logan had never seen. Usually the Professor seemed lost in whatever he was studying at the time, only coming up for air when he needed more blood. Logan hoped he wasn't out for blood at the moment. The Professor passed an icepack off to Diane and glared at Logan as he walked by.

Tah and Reno stood on the porch, waiting as the Professor stepped out with Logan right behind him.

"Sit," the Professor ordered, pointing to the chairs and lounger on the porch.

Logan moved immediately. Reno paused and looked at the Professor. He must have picked up on what Logan saw because Reno followed suit and sat in the chair across from Logan. Tah took a few minutes longer. Logan wondered for a minute if Tah was going to challenge the Professor, who was essentially a father-type figure for Abby. But Tah finally heaved a long sigh and sat.

"I have done nothing but offer support to all of you," the Professor began. "I open my home to you, give my labs over to help find answers for you. I do research and work long hours, for you. Not because I expect something in return, but because of my deep love for knowledge and understanding, and because that young woman in there is family to me. You think I stay here because my daughter asked me to or because I have nowhere else to go?" He shook his head. "I stay here because each and every one of you have come to mean something to me. I stay because the thought of leaving breaks my heart. Or it did. Until today. I am deeply ashamed of all three of you. I remember when you arrived here, a little battered, tired, but so filled with life and love for one another. You're the best of friends who chose to see each other as brothers. So where are those brothers now? Because, trust me, those are not the men I see sitting before me." He turned to Tah then. "You are the leader of this pride. I say pride, not just because it's what the technical term is for a group of cats or cat shifters but because this is a group of people to take pride in. Or it was. I know it's hard to find yourself thrust into a role you never knew existed, but it's yours. Now step up to the plate and be the leader you are, the leader you've always been. And a good leader sees the disquiet among his people and addresses it before these things happen."

He turned to Logan and Reno. Logan braced himself for what was coming.

"And you two. You disappoint me the most. At least Tah has the excuse of having a mate, who until very recently, looked like she was at death's door. The two of you… You have mates who are hurting, both of you, and both of them in similar ways. Reno, you think Amia has been through too much, and you fear for her. Your mate is a strong woman. She survived a living hell without you. I think she could walk through flames unharmed now that she has you. You need to see that, and allow her to see that, as well. You and your mate look at Clara, but you don't see her. Did you forget that Amia told you Clara had been buried alive as well when she was captured? After they tortured her? Yes, Amia rescued her, but Clara was only sixteen, as well. Plus, the things she's seen. So much death at the hands of men who are anything but human. I'm ashamed of the way we've treated her since she arrived. We fell into the same mold as those we call enemies. It makes us weak, and weakness will tear us apart." The Professor shook his head and sighed before glancing at Logan and holding his gaze. "Logan. I think I'm most disappointed in you."

Logan looked at him incredulously. Why was he the most disappointing?

"Tah and Reno…" The Professor shrugged. "They're warriors. But you, Logan. You're more than a warrior. Just as Abby is the heart of this pride, you are the heart of the three of you. You bring the laughter and the fun. You lost that at some point. I'm not sure if it was getting shot or if it was the slow recovery. I think you might find it again, with Clara. You will be a balm to her soul, freeing her from all the pain her past has held. Find the man you were and don't lose him again. We need him. All of us."

In that moment, the Professor looked incredibly tired and showed his age for the first time since Logan had met him. "Now I'm heading back to my lab so I can get some work done. And yes, vampire king that I am, I want all of you to stop down and give me some more blood. Suffice it to say, I need it. I may have something for you soon, something for all of us. I just need a few more tests before I'm sure enough to discuss it."

"We'll be there," Tah promised, standing and putting his hand on the Professor's shoulder.

Logan and Reno both stood. Reno nodded at the Professor with respect, but Logan moved close and embraced him.

"Thanks," Logan said. "Not just for this, but for all you do for us. Clara and I will stop down later. I know you said you wanted her saliva, as well."

The Professor stepped back, nodded and rubbed his eyes. For a split second, Logan was horrified the other man might cry.

"Abby is right," the Professor said. "We are family, and this family sticks together. No matter what gets thrown at us." He turned and walked into the house, leaving them standing on the porch.

Tah faced them both and held his hands up. "Okay. What do we do to fix this? Because we are going to fix this, and everybody is going to be fucking happy."

"I've got an idea," Logan said. "But first." He punched Reno hard in the arm.

"What the fuck?" Reno said.

"Just settling things up a bit," Logan said with a grin. "Be glad it wasn't your face. Now let's talk."

Chapter Nine

Clara watched Abby pace the room while she held an icepack to her cheek. Diane had brought it to her, saying the Professor had put it together for her. Then Diane had disappeared and left the three of them alone. Abby hadn't said a word yet. Clara glanced at her then toward Amia. Finally, she couldn't handle it anymore.

"I'm sorry," Clara told them both. "I've brought nothing but more confusion and chaos since I got here. That's the last thing I wanted. And hurting you," she said to Amia then turned to include Abby. "I never wanted to hurt either of you. I was trying to protect you."

"You saved my life," Abby said. "That's not adding to chaos and confusion. That's huge." Abby wrapped her arms around her belly. "I love my son, and I can't wait to welcome him into this world. You've just made it a lot easier for me to endure the end of this pregnancy before he gets here."

"I should have told you immediately," Clara said.

"When?" Abby asked softly. "Logan is absolutely right. When did we ever give you a chance to talk to us and tell us things? Certainly not when we had you facing a room full of strangers, yelling at you and demanding things from you. I'm ashamed of how we reacted. It wasn't right or fair."

"People are dying out there, Abby. I don't blame you for how I was greeted. I was essentially a stranger, one who followed Amia and Reno here without them being aware."

"We've done so much wrong," Abby stated. "Look at what happened with Amia. Then with you. We've turned into the beast. I want to believe like you do, Clara. That we can defeat the beast without becoming one."

Amia finally stood up and moved over to sit on the couch with Clara. Clara tensed up. She couldn't help herself, and Abby stopped and moved toward them.

"I'm sorry," Amia said. "I lost my head. I let the past pull me back and I just…I just snapped. I shouldn't have hit you. I'm so sorry."

"I should have told you when I got here. I should have told you when you came upstairs to talk."

"About that." Amia dropped her head and shook it back and forth. "Reno didn't realize what I was planning. Vic and I put the recorder in my phone before I went up. Reno knew I was planning to talk to you, but Vic didn't approach me about the phone idea until just before. We knew you wanted to make a call. You've yelled it for a week now. Vic thought we might find some answers if we let you. I agreed with her at the time. But I need Logan to know that Reno never betrayed his friendship. He wouldn't do that, and I would never ask him to."

"Logan and I didn't become mates until after I spoke to you, after you left the phone."

"That doesn't excuse it," Amia offered apologetically.

"What a mess," Clara said. "I can't imagine what it did to you to hear Lydia and have her say what she did."

"I always thought my mother loved me. No matter what I faced, I always had that little piece of warmth inside me. And now…now I know that she's been alive this whole time and written me off because of who my father is. And it all makes sense. I wondered every time Marcus would utter the words, blood will tell. I wondered why he kept me alive and didn't just kill me. I'd be an even more powerful lesson to others if I was tortured and killed. But I think I understand now."

"What are you thinking?" Abby asked, sitting on the other side of Clara.

"I think he expected me to find out she was alive and go to her, lead them to her. He expected her to come after me." She suddenly started laughing.

"What?" Clara asked, a little nervously. Was Amia losing it?

"You have to admit, it's funny. Both of them saying the same phrase, blood will tell, and meaning different things by it. Him thinking I was so much like her, and her afraid I was destined to be just like him."

"You're not," Clara said. "I've watched you. You're ruled by your heart, where they are both ruled by fear. I think it's one of the things that drew me to you and made me want to help you so badly. I called my uncle and Lydia when we were running, when you rescued me and left with me."

"You did?" Amia asked.

Clara nodded. "Your mom might say the things she does, but I remember when she dreamed of you and woke me up calling your name. It was a year before she could talk about you and tell me who you were. Thoughts of you tore her up. It's why I went to find you. Lydia was growing so sad, so distant from everyone around her, so consumed with a need for vengeance. I thought if I could just find you and bring you home, she'd see that things were okay."

"What happened?" Abby asked when Clara paused.

"Lydia went crazy. She swore bringing Amia back was the equivalent of putting a welcome sign up for the hunters. She was convinced we'd all die."

Amia wiped a tear off her face, and Clara gripped the other woman's hands tightly. "I wanted to bring you with me. I even thought about running with you and trying to find someplace we could both hide. But I was terrified. Finding you was my first trip away from home, and I almost got myself killed. How would I protect both of us?"

"I didn't know you thought about that," Amia said.

"I used to pretend you were my sister," Clara confessed. "I'd pretend you were away visiting family and would be home soon."

"You are sisters now," Abby intervened. "As the mates of Reno, Logan and Tah, we're all sisters." She heaved a heavy sigh and leaned back on the couch. "We need to be building our mates up, not tearing them apart."

"You're right," Amia said and glanced back at Clara. "I shouldn't blame you for things you had no control over. Do you know what happened the night Lydia ran to you?"

"My father had been captured that day. Lydia admitted you could see a shifter's glow, the warmth of the animal we hold inside. She said you told her my father glowed and so she went to try and save him. She couldn't, though. They'd pinned him to the wall with bolts." Clara shuddered and pushed to her feet, needing a little space before she could continue. "They'd stabbed him in the stomach. He knew he was dying."

"Clara, my God," Abby said with a shake of her head.

"He sent her away, but she didn't make it out in time," Clara continued. "There was a boy watching." She glanced at Amia.

"Kellan," Amia whispered.

Clara nodded. "He beat Lydia up pretty badly and left her there while he went to call Marcus. Lydia said that was when my dad told her about us and how to reach us. She said she went to get you, but Kellan was there, and she couldn't. I think she convinced herself leaving you was the right choice to make by repeating to herself that you're a Blane. I think she did it to try to keep her sanity and instead, it drove her insane. I really believe she loves you so much that leaving you destroyed part of her."

Amia was crying. Abby was crying. And Clara knew she had tears on her own cheeks, as well.

"I need to tell you something. Both of you. I've been so unsure of what to say and how to say it and that's why I really wanted to call my Uncle Thomas."

"There's nothing you can't tell us," Abby stated.

"That's where you're wrong," Clara countered. "I can tell you all the medical knowledge I know, though I think there's someone better to get that from. I can also tell you what I know about hunters. I think Amia and I could both help with that as we've both been on the receiving end of a hunter's agenda. But there are things I can't tell you, Abby. I may not have heard of the legend you mentioned to me, but I have heard of Tah. I've spent my whole life searching for him, only I was looking for someone much older and better informed, someone to educate me."

"So you have heard something of the legend. I knew it!" Abby said excitedly. "You've just heard it described differently."

"I can tell you one thing," Clara confessed. "The Tah I was expecting is not the man I met. He is, but he isn't. I see the leader within him. But right now that leader is limited by what he doesn't know. And that scares me. I've always heard of how the Tah will come and save us all. Now? I'm not sure that's going to happen. I'm not sure of anything anymore."

"But this is fantastic news," Abby gushed. "I was right. We were right. This means more shifters will come. They'll find him. They'll have to. And together, maybe all of us can save each other. You don't need Tah to save you, neither of you do. You saved yourselves. But Tah can be that beacon to people who need one. My mate is strong and fierce and unafraid of doing what is right, what is just. He's smart and brave and loving. He's everything you need him to be and so much more. He's so much more." She pushed up off the couch and began pacing the room. "We need to clean more rooms up, get this place in shape. Pack in more supplies. They'll be coming, and we'll be waiting to welcome them home."

Abby practically gushed with enthusiasm and excitement. Tah's blood had obviously been the elixir of life she'd required. Clara was glad she'd known to have them give Abby a transfusion.

"She's a little scary in this mode," Amia whispered, rising and coming up beside Clara.

Clara nodded and glanced down when Amia laced their fingers and squeezed.

"I always wanted sisters," Amia said.

Clara blinked rapidly to keep the fresh tears at bay. "Me, too."

"We're going to be okay," Amia whispered, and Clara nodded.

"We're going to be better than okay," Abby said, letting them know she'd heard every word they'd said. "Soon this house will spill over with people. Our family is growing, ladies. So we better get our shit together and be ready for what's coming."

* * * *

"Hold up," Zane ordered, pushing Murphy back. "Go in smart, not with emotion overwhelming you. You want to get us all fucking killed?"

"You said he was dying. What the fuck do you want me to do? I'm going in there and saving my brother's ass," Murphy hissed quietly.

"Not half-cocked, you won't." Zane bent down so he was nose-to-nose with Murphy. "You will be calm. You will be smart. We are no good to anyone if we're captured and killed. You have to think, Murphy. Open your senses. Tell me what you feel, what you smell."

Murphy glared for a moment before closing his eyes. "Well, move back then or all I'll smell is your arrogance."

Zane grunted and stepped back. He was curious to see how well trained Murphy was. He knew the other man was a shifter, as well, but did he know how to link his abilities so they were accessible as man or beast?

Murphy inhaled. "I smell sweat, cigarettes and stale coffee. Blood. Theirs and his. I feel anger, hate and something else. Curiosity, maybe? Something is off. I smell." He blinked his eyes open and met Zane's hard stare. "I smell a shifter. A shifter is here or was here. What the hell is going on here?"

"I don't know, Murph, and that's why we need to be smart about this. I'll go in there with you, and if today is the day I die, then I'm ready. But being ready doesn't mean I'm just going to walk in blind. Now, are you ready to discuss this logically?"

Murphy nodded. "I smell so many scents, outside of the shifter and the hunters. God, the stench of blood is thick…so thick. It makes it hard to weed through. I can't tell if the scents are fresh or older."

"What do you feel? Are you still connected to Finn?"

"Yes. It's weak. I'm cold and that scares me more than being numb. But he's still here."

"We go in low and quiet. Keep your senses open no matter how overwhelming the blood is. No more than twelve feet between us at any given time. And do not run into anything, even if you see Finn. It could always be a trap."

"I'm good now," Murphy promised. "My head is clear, but we need to go. I can feel him fading, Zane. My brother's dying."

"Go," Zane said and moved to follow. "Jesus!" he muttered under his breath. "Tah is going to kill us if we survive this."

They moved silently through the wooded area where Murphy's link with Finn had led them. The pain had proven to be a better beacon than the phone. Zane still found it a little odd that the two brothers shared a connection that he'd only heard of happening with mates. But who knew? It would be something to discuss with his uncle when he had the opportunity.

Zane emptied his mind and concentrated on his surroundings and on Murphy moving in front of him. The scent of blood was nauseating. It coated everything and made Zane afraid of what they might find. He prayed for strength to help Murphy if it was as bad as he feared. Finn might only be holding on until his brother arrived.

Murphy stopped and motioned for Zane to move up and join him. Zane squatted next to him in the trees and took in the clearing in front of them. There was a cabin that looked as if it was one good breeze from falling over. There were a couple of sleeping bags out front and a fire that had burned down to embers. But something wasn't right. This close, the scent of death overpowered that of blood.

'Murphy,' he mouthed and shook his head.

Murphy gave him a sad look, and Zane could literally feel the waves of pain coming off the other man. Murphy moved quickly at a low crouch from the tree line toward the closest sleeping bag. He had his hand over the person's mouth and was dragging him out almost as soon as he reached him.

Zane followed, staying low and moving toward the bag on the opposite side. The first thing he noticed was how neither of the people moved. Then he noticed why. Murphy glanced over at him and mouthed that his guy was dead. Zane nodded and indicated to the one at his feet. The man there was dead, as well. Zane took a closer look. Hell, the cut across the guy's neck was so deep he was almost decapitated.

Murphy crept closer to the cabin, head turning side-to-side as he seemed to pick up on a scent. A deep growl rumbled from his massive chest, and he moved around the cabin. Zane made the choice to trust him to look out for himself and, instead of following, he carefully opened the cabin door. More blood. It was everywhere. Splattered on the floor and walls. It was a fucking blood bath. Jesus! What the hell had happened here?

He found two more bodies crumpled like rag dolls just inside the door. The sparse furniture that had been inside was overturned and obscured part of the floor from Zane's line of sight. This more than explained the scent of blood. But where was Finn? He ducked his head back out the door to check on Murphy real quick. The other man was just coming around the corner.

"Found another one back there. Neck slit deep just like these two," Murphy said with a nod toward the sleeping bags. "One in the back has Finn's blood on him as well. It's strong."

"I found two more bodies inside the door here. Looks like most of the killing took place there. I haven't found Finn."

Murphy took a deep breath and peered around Zane into the cabin. "He's in here. I can feel him." He rubbed his arms as if gripped by a cold only he felt. "Help me move some of this stuff. I thought he was behind the cabin. He must be in the back somewhere."

Zane stepped in to help Murphy right the table and move stuff around. He noticed another body toward the rear of the cabin, shoved halfway under the bed. Murphy must have seen it at the same time. He gave a cry and headed over to it, dropping to his knees and moaning as he tugged it free. But it wasn't Finn. It was another man with his head nearly cut off.

"Where the fuck is he?" Murphy roared, and Zane prayed luck was with them and no one was left around to hear them.

A moan sounded from under the bed. Murphy tossed it aside as if it was nothing more than kindling, which it was when it hit the wall and splintered. Finn was on his back in the far corner.

"Mur…phy…"

"I'm here, brother. I'm here."

Zane moved to join them when he heard the moan resonate in Murphy's throat. He caught his breath, as well. Finn was naked, his body riddled with bruises and cuts. His face was swollen and distorted beyond recognition. They'd obviously tortured the hell out of him. But then what had happened? How did they all die? There was no way Finn had been able to do it. Hell his hands were purple and swollen, and Zane would bet anything they'd broken every bone in his fingers. There was no way Finn had been able to make a cut as deep as the ones on the bodies around him.

"Jesus, Finn. What happened to you?" Murphy asked as he wrapped his arm under Finn and eased him up in his arms.

Finn groaned. "Hurts," he slurred. "Dy…ing…"

"Shh," Murphy scolded and Zane saw tears flowing down his cheeks. "We're going to get you out of here. You're going to be fine, just fine. You can't leave me. Who's going to watch over me? You know my temper. Besides, Molly will hunt me down and kill me if you up and die on us."

Zane moved a little ways away and opened his phone. He thought for a few minutes and hit the number to dial straight into the lab. He knew who would answer.

"Hello?" Diane's voice came over the line, calm and sure, just like she always seemed. Those were two of the qualities he liked most about her.

"It's Zane. We found Finn. He's bad, Diane. I'm not sure he'll last the trip back."

"How bad?"

"I think it's safe to say he's dying," he whispered.

"Oh, God."

"Diane?" Zane called. He could hear her talking to someone in the background.

"How bad is he?" the Professor asked, coming on the line.

"I don't think he's going to make it," Zane told him.

"Listen to me," the Professor said quietly. "I need you to get him in the car and get back here as soon as you can. I'll be waiting for you. Drive straight through. Don't stop unless you absolutely have to. Where are you?"

"New Mexico," Zane answered.

"Damn it!" the Professor yelled. "Tell Murphy to keep him alive. Whatever he needs to do. Just get Finn here alive."

"He won't make it through a surgery," Zane said.

"It's not surgery I have in mind. I've been working on something. Just get him here, Zane, and I'll do my best to save him."

Chapter Ten

Logan took Clara's hand and led her out of the front room where everyone not on patrol had gathered. Reno and Amia, along with Vic were out walking the perimeters and checking the alarms they'd placed. Kenzie was in the control room with Holt. Abby and the Professor were poring over the information Jess had sent them. Tah paced back and forth and Diane stood at the window, glancing between the clock and the outside. Logan couldn't take it anymore.

"We'll be back," he told the room at large.

Tah waved him off and kept right on pacing. It would be a long night as they waited for Zane to get there with Murphy and Finn. Tah was blaming himself as were Reno and Amia. Here they were just starting to settle the dust from one rough patch and they were already being slammed with something else. Something even bigger. Yet again it seemed as if they could lose one of their own.

Zane had called the lab first, speaking to Diane then the Professor. He'd called Tah as Diane was coming up the stairs to let them know what was going on. From what Logan gathered, Zane believed Finn had been taken by hunters. But that wasn't all. Someone had killed all of the men and left Finn for dead. They wouldn't know what had happened until Finn could talk and tell them, if he made it. Zane had told Tah he'd taken a few pictures real quick before they high-tailed it out of there.

"Where are we going?" Clara whispered as they walked away. "Are you okay?"

"I need some space," Logan admitted, tugging her toward the stairs. "And I've been wanting to talk to you all day."

He stopped outside the door to their room and ran his fingers softly over the bruise on her cheek. "I should have hit Reno harder," he said and turned to push open the door and urge her inside.

"Wait," Clara said. "You hit Reno? What were you thinking?"

"That he deserved it?" Logan offered. "It was a love tap. He won't be sporting a bruise."

"Logan, Amia was reacting in the moment. Finding out about Lydia the way she did, it was a lot to take in," Clara told him. "She and I are okay now."

"Reno and I are, as well. In fact, I've talked him and Tah into a celebration of sorts, or at least I had before all this came up with Finn and Murphy. God, it will kill Tah and Reno if Finn doesn't make it. They'll always blame themselves."

"Why? And what celebration?" Clara asked.

"Tah will feel guilty because he told Finn to watch Amia while he talked to Reno. Finn overheard Amia telling Reno she was going to kill him and then all of us."

"What?"

"It was before you arrived. Thing is, Amia meant it figuratively, not literally. But Finn didn't know that."

"She assumed the Blanes would find her and in the process, find all of you."

"Bingo," Logan agreed. "So Reno blasted Finn and probably thinks that's why Finn took off with the transmitter that was put in Amia."

"You don't think it was?" Clara asked.

"Who knows?" Logan said with a shrug. "I've learned not to read into what you see or think you know. I think we've had enough of that around here." He turned her into his arms and tugged her against his chest. "But I didn't bring you up here to talk about all that."

"You didn't?" She smiled up at him.

"I need you, Clara. I need to feel you against me. To hold you close. To make love to you."

"All you ever have to do is say the word, Logan. I promise you, I'll always want you just as much."

"Always?" he asked, reaching down to grip the edge of her shirt and pulling it over her head.

"You're my mate. As soon as I'm around you, I feel your desire, your want, and it becomes my own."

"Is it always like that?" he asked, cupping her breasts over her bra and rubbing his thumbs over her nipples. "Do mates always fall in love with one another?"

She nodded. "I've never seen it not happen. But you have to understand. It's not just about biology. We connect on an emotional level far deeper than the average human couple can. I know your thoughts and emotions better than even Reno or Tah, even though I've known you for a shorter time. It's the way we bond, sharing feelings with one another. It unites us. I can't feel your pain without hurting. I can't feel your joy without smiling. And I can't feel the things you feel for me when you look at me like that, and not give them back."

Logan smiled at her. "You love me," he said and bent to kiss her lips before she could reply.

He knew it. If she felt what he was feeling, then it was inevitable. Obviously, the fates knew what they were about with this mate thing. They seemed to fall hard, fast. The first time Clara had looked at him in the lab, he'd felt the zing of that shared glance all the way to his heart. She'd stepped in front of him, as if to protect him. No woman had ever done anything like that for him. Then he'd touched her and it was as if every inch of his body had become supercharged for her, all for her.

"Let's get these off of you." He reached around and unhooked her bra, letting her do the honors while he slid his hands lower to her pants.

Soon they were a tangle of hands and half-removed clothing. He wasn't sure how they managed it but eventually they were both naked.

"My turn," Clara told him and gave him a shove onto the bed.

He landed on the edge and threw his hands out to clench the covers when she dropped to her knees between his thighs.

"I've been thinking about this all day," she purred and leaned in to lick the thick shaft of his cock.

"Jesus, woman." Logan grunted, bringing one hand up to cup the back of her head. "You feel good."

She nuzzled against him, brushing her nose over his flesh and inhaling while she flicked her tongue out again and again. She cupped his ball sac with one hand and wrapped the fingers of her other one around his shaft, pumping them up and down. She flicked that wicked golden glance of hers up to clash with his and rubbed her tongue over the crown of his dick.

"Clara." He groaned, knowing he was on the edge and wouldn't be able to take much more teasing from her. "Either suck my cock or get that pretty little ass up here and fuck me."

She grinned up at him and raked those sharp canines of hers against his groin. His cock pulsed and a drop of pre-cum filled the slit on the head. She ran her tongue over it, licking it off and moaning in pleasure. He was never going to last at this rate.

"Suck it," he demanded and rocked his hips up toward her.

His cock missed her mouth and skimmed along her cheek instead. She turned and nuzzled his shaft again, flicking her quick little tongue over and around him.

"Clara," he pleaded.

With a moan she took him deep. No playing around this time. She wrapped those lush lips around his cock and sucked it to the back of her throat, swallowed, then pulled back until he brushed the roof of her mouth. She swirled, licked, sucked and swallowed, and never in the same pattern. It kept him right on the edge, not knowing what she would do next. It was the best fucking blowjob of his life.

"Ahhh, God, baby," he told her. "You feel so fucking good." He had both hands clenched by his hips again, fighting the urge to fuck her sweet mouth with his cock.

She made some small sound and it vibrated all down his shaft until he felt it in his balls. She did it again and he was panting with the effort to keep from shooting his load in her mouth. He wasn't ready for this pleasure to end. She peeked up at him through her lashes and her cheeks hollowed out as she increased the suction. The hand cupping his balls slid back and he almost came off the bed when she pressed two fingers against the skin just behind his ball sac.

"Fuck!" he shouted, as every muscle in his body seemed to lock down. "I'm coming, baby. I'm coming."

The vixen only worked his dick harder, tapping her tongue along the underside of his cockhead until the first splash of seed left him. He watched her throat work as she swallowed it down and felt her tongue licking over the crown as the next jet of semen left. She took it and pulled back, wrapping her lips around the bulging head and sucking only it, as if she were greedy for more of his cum.

He collapsed on the bed, his body shaking from the orgasm she'd given him. He couldn't feel anything but the racing of his heart and the soft puffs of her breath against his spent cock. Good, God, the woman was fucking incredible!

"Come here," he murmured and patted his chest.

His eyes were closed but he felt her moving up, using his thigh to help her rise from her knees. Her body brushed along his as she joined him on the bed. She kissed his shoulder, his chest then nibbled along his jaw.

"I think I just found my new favorite treat," she said and smacked her lips together.

He chuckled. "I think I can survive more of that. Lord, woman! I'm not sure how long it will take me to recover though. You are by far the sexiest woman I've ever met in my life."

"You're welcome," she said with a purr in her throat again.

He wanted to hear that sound often from her. It made his chest swell with pride, as if he'd done something incredibly right instead of just lucking into being the mate of this magnificent woman.

Finally catching his breath and feeling as if his blood flow was back to normal and not centered on his dick, Logan sat up and pressed her down onto her back on the bed. "My turn."

She grinned and wiggled up with excitement clear on her face. "Why, Logan. I thought you'd never offer."

He laughed and dropped his mouth down to hers. "Offer's always on the table," he whispered against her lips then kissed her.

Her hands came up to cup his face, and he took the kiss deeper than he'd first planned. It was like that with her. He didn't think a lifetime together would be long enough to sate his need for her. Being mated was the best thing in the world. Being mated to Clara was beyond compare to anything. He was one lucky bastard, and he knew it.

He broke the kiss and immediately slid down to the rounded curves of her breasts. She wasn't overly large, and he liked that. She fit his hands perfectly and those pert nipples of hers were made for sucking. He licked over her then brushed his closed lips along the underside of her breasts, nuzzled the sides and licked over the tight buds again. Back and forth he went, never staying at one breast too long, never giving one nipple too much attention.

She was shifting her legs restlessly on the bed, and he knew if he slid a hand lower she'd be nice and wet for him.

"Logan."

Her fingers clenched in his hair and held him in place when he would have moved over to the other breast. He chuckled against the nipple before opening up and grazing it with his teeth. She moaned and the hair on his scalp prickled from the sharp clasp of her fingers. He gripped the nipple with his teeth and tugged at it, shifting one hand over to allow him to use his fingers to do the same to the other one.

She was panting now, moaning in pleasure as she rubbed her thighs together. He knew what she wanted, what she needed. He sucked the plump berry into his mouth and plied it with his teeth and tongue while he used his fingers on the other. And she came apart under him, not needing his touch or hers between her legs to help her along.

"Inside me," she panted. "I need you inside me."

"Not yet," he murmured against her skin as he skimmed his lips over her, moving lower.

Her stomach trembled beneath his touch, and he stopped to dip his tongue into her belly button, enjoying the way she shivered. He moved so his body was between her thighs, pressing them wider as he slid his shoulders down so his mouth was poised over the flushed lips of her pussy. She was wet from her orgasm and the small pearl of her clit was just peeking out at him, as if it was too shy to ask for what it wanted. But he knew. He knew exactly what he wanted to do.

He flicked his tongue out and licked over her pussy, zeroing in on where her juices were thickest. He lapped at her, loving the musky essence of her. Sweet. She was so sweet, like hot, fresh syrup. He worked his tongue up her lips, licking over them and sliding between them, tasting every part of her pink perfection before greeting her clit with a lover's kiss. She arched her hips off the bed, pressing into him while clawing the bed and shouting. She made him feel invincible.

He eased up and finally released her clit, immediately returning to her opening and thrusting his tongue as far in as he could get it. He changed the shape of his tongue, rounding it out then turning it back and forth inside her as he pumped it up into her channel. Another cry from her lips and her thighs were closing around his head, covering his ears so everything sounded as if he was inside a tunnel. Still, he teased her.

He ran one hand back up to toy with her clit while using the other to press against one thigh, getting her to ease the clamp she had on his head. He lifted a bit, glancing up her body to see her thrashing, hands cupping her breasts, fingers playing with her nipples while she moaned in pleasure. He thrust two fingers deep inside her and watched as her eyes flew open and she pinched down on her nipples.

"Yes!" she cried. "Oh, God, yes!"

She pumped her hips up into his penetration, and he added the flick of his tongue to the sensation of his finger over her clit. And enjoyed the site of making his woman come. She held nothing back, taking her pleasure the same way she gave it. Her neck arched back, lifting her chest high while her hips pressed deeper into the bed. His fingers were drenched with her juices and still he kept fucking her, kept rubbing his tongue against her, seeing how high she could go.

His cock was rock hard again, primed and ready to make love. He eased his fingers from the tight grip of her cunt and lowered his mouth to give her one more deep kiss before pulling away. He stood up, looking down at where she lay gasping for air, her body flushed from orgasm. Her nipples were hard points and her pussy lips were even plumper and wetter than before. As he watched, her eyes flicked open and those golden brown orbs of hers met his. She skimmed her gaze down to his bobbing erection and smiled.

Holding her hand out to him, she offered him everything. "Come here. Make love with me."

He turned her on the bed and joined her, moving between her thighs and slipping his cock into place. With one thrust, he buried his shaft completely inside her, loving the way her pussy felt as if it had been made for him and him alone. He wondered if she felt the same about his cock. He rocked into her, and she met him, matching his rhythm until they moved in tandem.

Their eyes met again, and he loved the way she smiled so softly at him, the way her hand skimmed up his side to grip his shoulder. The way her other hand slid down to cup his hip. And there it was, that swelling in his heart. And he knew with perfect clarity, he wasn't falling in love. He was already there.

* * * *

Diane was on the porch before Zane had even turned off the four-wheeler. Tah, Abby and the Professor spilled out after her. Reno, Amia and Vic came in from the woods as if they'd been watching for their arrival as well. Zane had a feeling they were just going to get the chance to say goodbye. Finn was fading fast. They were lucky he'd made it this far.

Zane moved to help Murphy slide off the back since the other man held Finn cradled in his arms. Zane was surprised when Diane came to him first, her hands brushing over him and setting his skin on fire. Tah and the others closed ranks around Murphy, helping him get Finn into the house.

"Are you hurt? Did you sustain any injuries?" She was worried. It carried through in her tone and shone for all to see in her eyes.

"I'm fine," he told her. Better than fine if her interest in him meant that his time of waiting might be over.

Their gazes met and held. He saw fear, uncertainty and just maybe the start of something more. Then she was moving from him, running into the house to catch up with the others, who were taking Finn down to the labs.

Abby turned to Zane and held her hand out. Her fingers were warm and firm as he took them in his.

"It's good to have you all home again," she told him.

"You look better," he said. "What changed?"

"Blood transfusion. I'll tell you all about it later. Clara was a Godsend. She knew just what I needed to help me through this. This little guy and I are going to be just fine." Abby brushed her free hand over her belly, and Zane couldn't help but smile.

He sobered quickly as they entered the house, and he saw them carrying Finn down the stairs to the labs as Zane had suspected.

"Should I call the rest in? Give them a chance to say goodbye?" he asked.

"Not just yet. The Professor has been working on something with all the blood he's been taking from everyone. If Murphy agrees, we might be able to help Finn, maybe even save his life."

Zane looked at Abby to see if she was serious. Her expression said she was. His curiosity piqued, he followed more quickly, not wanting to miss anything.

"Hurry," the Professor ordered. "Get him on the table. Get that shirt completely off him. Rip it if you must. I need to see how bad his injuries are to know what measures to take."

Murphy and Tah both moved to follow his command while Reno stayed close to offer help if needed. Zane knew all three men had to be blaming themselves for what Finn was going through. Zane was more of the opinion Finn had no one to blame but himself. His choice, his consequences. That was the way life worked.

"Dy…ing…" Finn managed to push the words out again, though Zane knew Finn was seriously weak. Dying? Hell, he should have been dead at this point. Zane had never expected to make it back with him alive.

Diane moved in and skimmed those long fingers of hers over Finn's stomach. She used a cloth to wipe away most of the blood so she could get a better look, but Zane could have told her it would only be replaced by more.

"Oh, shit, he's lost a lot of blood. I can't tell how deep this is, but it's still seeping out pretty steadily," she whispered and turned to the Professor. "If we're going to do this, we're going to have to do it now."

"Do what?" Murphy asked. "Can you save him or not?"

"Maybe," the Professor said slowly, his gaze on Tah. "I've been working with the blood. Well, part of it," he said with a wave of his hand. "I had an idea when Logan was shot. It took him so much longer to heal than it did Tah, simply because of the unique healing properties of Tah's shifter DNA. So I took blood and ran tests. I took more blood and ran more tests."

"Spit it out," Tah ordered.

"I've been working on a booster of sorts for the humans among us. Sort of a way to help them heal faster or to at least stabilize them in cases of more serious injuries until we can get them into surgery. But it's still in the testing stages. I'm not sure how it will work in reality, only in concept."

"Use it," Murphy said. "Test it on him."

"Murphy…" Tah began.

"No!" Murphy interrupted. "Fuck anything else." He turned pleading eyes to the Professor. "Save him. Please, don't let him die on me."

The Professor looked at Tah. "I won't do it without your okay."

"You certainly created it without my knowledge or my okay," Tah fired back. He shook his head and looked up. "Fuck," he muttered.

"Tah." Abby stepped up to her mate and took his hand. "The Professor was going over some of it with me earlier, while we were sitting on the couch. This is a great idea. Look at him." She pointed to where Finn lay, barely hanging on to consciousness. "We have to try."

"And what about the consequences? Do we even have an idea of what the side effects of this might be?"

"Not yet," the Professor admitted. "I just started testing it."

"On who?" Tah demanded.

"No one," the Professor admitted. "I've added it to some of the human blood I've got on hand. I have a program that runs, testing it and checking for any anomalies that might occur."

"Fuck!" Tah exploded again. "So we have no idea if we're attempting to save him or just killing him more painfully. And if this works and he pulls through, we have no idea what this could do to him."

"As next of kin, I give my okay. We'll deal with anything that happens when it happens. I just want him alive to deal with it," Murphy said.

Zane didn't envy Tah at that moment. Ultimately, the decision lay with him no matter what Murphy wanted, and they all knew it. Tah looked at Murphy and finally sighed. Zane could see the answer in his eyes.

"Do it," Tah told the Professor.

They moved quickly, and Zane was amazed all over again at how well the Professor and Diane worked together. They made it seem as if they'd known each other for longer than the months they'd all been here. She had a hand on Finn's elbow and a vein picked out by the time the Professor was back with the injection.

"I'm going to give him a shot first. This is a precisely measured quantity of the formula I've concocted. It's a fairly strong dose of the serum I'm working on. It should fire through his system and start increasing his healing immediately. I'm not sure how much his body will do on its own and how much will be left for us. We'll have to watch and see. We need to give this time to work. The time will depend on Finn and how he reacts to it."

Diane moved to the cabinets and started pulling stuff out while the Professor slowly pressed the golden fluid from the needle into Finn's vein.

"As soon as it's safe, we'll hook up an IV and put a more diluted version of this into him. From there, it will be a waiting game. I don't want to do anything to interfere while this is working." Finally he looked up and met Murphy's eyes. "There's one more thing you need to know, Tah. Do you want to tell him or should I?" the Professor asked Murphy.

Murphy gritted his teeth and glared at the Professor. Zane waited for it. If the Professor had been testing all their blood, then he knew who was shifter and who wasn't. Zane had figured as much, but as it hadn't appeared the Professor was going to give them away, he hadn't worried over it. Not that Tah didn't suspect with Zane, but Murphy was a different story. Now it looked as if the Professor was going to call them out.

Murphy glanced over at Tah. "I'm a shifter," he blurted. "Eurasian Lynx."

"Damn," Zane said. "I didn't know there were any more like you still around."

"I'm the last," Murphy said with a sad look on his face.

Tah glanced at Zane and lifted a brow.

"Now wait a minute," the Professor interrupted. "I had a reason for asking Murphy to speak up. No one else has to share anything they're not ready for.

Tah glared at the Professor again.

"It's okay. I think most of you already suspect I'm a shifter. You're right. I carry the spirit of a panther," Zane admitted to them, his glance skimming over to Diane. He didn't see revulsion on her face. That was a good sign, since he was just about done hiding from her. It was becoming too much to fight the urge to claim what the beast within knew was his.

"Why did Tah need to know about Murphy?" Abby asked.

"Just in case," the Professor mumbled.

"In case of what?" Murphy and Tah asked at the same time.

"Finn is Murphy's biological brother. He also carries a unique DNA code just as you do, Murphy."

"Shifter DNA?" Murphy asked.

"Yes," the Professor admitted.

"How is that possible?" Tah asked.

"How is any of what we've seen possible?" the Professor countered. "It is what it is. Finn has shifter DNA. His is just recessive…for now. I'm not sure if this serum will change that or not."

"You mean this could awaken the shifter part of him?" Abby asked.

"I honestly don't know," the Professor said. "All we can do is watch."

"Well, fuck," Murphy said, then surprised them all by laughing. "He's always said he should have been the shifter, said he'd be better at it than me. The crazy son of a bitch might just get his wish."

Chapter Eleven

Clara woke up refreshed and feeling better than she had in a long time. Logan had woken her once during the night. He'd gone down to check on Finn, Murphy and Zane and come back up with an unbelievable tale of what the Professor had come up with. A serum that used shifter DNA to boost a human's healing capabilities? Clara was certain that wasn't something they wanted to get out. They might be hunted for other reasons then, by countless others.

Logan was already gone, but she found a note on her pillow telling her how beautiful she looked sleeping and that he'd gone to take early patrol. He also said he'd be running into town later and invited her to go along. That really made her grin. It would be almost like a date, which was really funny when she thought about it. They'd pretty much done everything at this point, except go on a date.

She hurriedly threw on clothes, brushed her teeth and hair then headed downstairs to see who was around. Her palms were a little sweaty, and her heart beat a little faster than normal, but her nerves were explainable after all that had gone down.

"Good morning," Abby called out to her as Clara passed the front room in search of the kitchen. "Where are you off to?"

"The kitchen if I can find it," Clara admitted. "I'm starving."

"Me, too," Abby agreed with a smile and linked arms with her, walking with Clara toward the kitchen. "I swear since I got that infusion of Tah's blood, my appetite has doubled."

"You were growing weaker, which means the baby would have eventually grown weaker, as well," Clara said. "After he'd depleted you of everything. Both of you needed the boost from Tah's blood. Shifters carry a unique hormone that isn't shared with our mates. But it's that hormone that is needed during pregnancy. Not a big deal if the woman is a shifter, but if she's human…" Clara shrugged. "Well, you've seen and felt what that is like."

"Yes," Abby agreed with a laugh. "Thanks, but no thanks! I much prefer how I'm feeling now."

They walked into the kitchen and Abby started pointing and talking.

"We keep all the staples on hand. There's fresh fruit, cereal, oatmeal, frozen waffles, eggs, bacon and yogurt. If you like something we don't have, you put it on the list and we'll see if it's in town next trip. We usually go once a week for little stuff, and every two weeks for major things. We cook in rotation, which you'll be added to now. Hope you know how to cook. If not, I'm sure you can sucker Logan into helping. That man is phenomenal in the kitchen."

"Logan cooks?" Clara asked.

"Like a master chef," Abby stated and hummed. "I'll admit to using this pregnancy to con Logan into cooking for me. Tah's passable. Reno burns everything. Zane is probably as good as Logan. The rest of us do a good enough job. We keep the Professor out of here."

"He can't cook?"

"He can cook," Abby said. "He just forgets what he's doing and tends to walk away while stuff is cooking. Not a great thing."

"Logan told me about the experimental injections the Professor's been working on. That's amazing to have someone with that type of knowledge on your side. I wish my Uncle Thomas were here. They'd get along wonderfully."

"Your uncle is a scientist?" Abby asked.

"He's actually a doctor, but one created through necessity not schooling."

"There was a need, and he found a way to fulfill it?" Abby asked.

Clara nodded as she pulled a couple of bowls down and grabbed a box of granola cereal. "My dad and my uncle have always provided a safe haven for our kind. We have a sort of..." She thought, searching for a way to describe it. "I guess maybe a type of underground railroad for lack of a better description. Those who need it know how to find it."

"We wouldn't have had a clue," Abby said.

"But then, you didn't really need it," Clara offered with a shrug. "Look at you. You've got this fortress in the middle of nowhere, and plenty of people to watch your back."

"It's the Professor's. He says he had it built a long time ago and just kept adding on to it over the years. The generators are unbelievable. And he's even talking about doing more. His money is tied up at the moment. Jess and I are dealing with the attorneys on it."

"Why is it tied up?" Clara asked, then added, "Jess is his daughter?"

"Yes. It's tied up because as far as the rest of the world is concerned, Professor Mueller is dead, killed in an explosion. Jess and her mates did it to protect him from whatever they're facing."

"Wolves are less social than cats," Clara offered. "They tend to stay in smaller groups and don't mix with other shifters, even other breeds of wolves. They're a different lot."

"So that's why you couldn't help the ones Amia freed from the Blanes," Abby said.

"Yeah." Clara nodded, setting the two bowls she'd grabbed together on the table. "Here, eat with me, so I don't feel so bad for sleeping in."

Abby laughed and joined her at the table. "Wow, this looks good. What did you mix in here?"

"Some fresh fruit, granola cereal and yogurt. I could seriously live off this stuff."

Abby took a bite and moaned at the taste while Clara watched with a grin. "I can see why. Mhmm. Looks like you get to make me breakfast for a while."

Clara laughed. "No problem, unless I get an early rotation like Logan."

"I might have some pull on that," Abby promised, eating another bite. "So I'm curious, are there other shifters?"

"Well, yeah. There are lots of cats out there," Clara said, giving Abby a weird look.

"I mean other shifters outside of cats and wolves," Abby clarified.

Clara shrugged. "I've never seen any, but that doesn't mean anything. Shifters, like humans, are social creatures, but we tend to flock to those we share things in common with. So it only makes sense that any others would stick with those like them, whatever that is."

"I guess," Abby agreed. "I'm just naturally curious."

"Logan said something about a celebration?" Clara asked.

"I think it's a great idea," Abby enthused. "We haven't celebrated anything since we've been here. We've gotten so wrapped up in learning and protecting, and that's not bad. It was a very necessary thing, but now? We need to remember there is life outside of all this turmoil. We need to remember to laugh, to just have fun. We need moments like that maybe more now than ever before. I'm glad Logan thought of it. He's planning a trip into town later to pick some stuff up for it. I'm sure he'll cook."

Clara laughed. "Now I'll be looking forward to that after the glowing endorsement you gave him."

"Are you going into town with him?"

"I think so," Clara said. "He left me a note before he headed out this morning, telling me he was going and inviting me along."

Abby's face lit up. "Will you do me a favor?"

"Sure? Do you need something?"

"Tah said Logan used to play the guitar, said he was amazing, but he hasn't picked one up in years. Reno said Logan left his guitar behind when Reno was shot outside a bar." Abby waved her hand. "That was before I met them, before any of this started. Anyway, it was gone when Logan went back for it."

"Wow. I heard you say they'd all been shot. I thought maybe Reno was shot by hunters, as well, but his was before all this?"

Abby nodded. "He stepped in when a woman was being attacked and was shot."

"So he's always been a savior of sorts," Clara said with a smile, thinking of how happy Amia was now with Reno.

"I think they all have been," Abby said then got back to her request. "I'd love to hear Logan play and since we're having a celebration—it just seems like the perfect time."

"Logan didn't tell me he played," Clara admitted softly.

"Don't let it bother you," Abby said, reaching over and patting her hand. "I still learn new things about Tah all the time. And Reno and Amia? They're still getting to know things about each other, too. This mating thing is crazy with how fast it moves you into a physical relationship. Everything is intense from the very beginning," Abby said with a smile and rubbed her belly. "But I wouldn't change it for anything."

"Me, either," Clara agreed.

"Hey, there you are," Logan said as he walked into the kitchen.

Clara couldn't help but admire the way he looked in his well-worn jeans and form-fitting T-shirt. His sandy brown hair was just long enough to curl under at his neck and those deep brown eyes of his were like warm molasses this morning. As he crossed to her, she felt her heart swell with pride as her whole body acknowledged that he was hers.

He stopped beside her and leaned in to kiss her softly on the lips. "Mhmm," he murmured. "You taste like strawberries and bananas."

"Breakfast," she said, indicating the bowls before her and Abby.

"Yummy," he said and leaned in for a deeper taste. She knew her nipples were poking against her shirt when he finally pulled back, and she saw the look of possessive delight in his eyes.

She could tell they were both thinking the same thing, and they were both right.

Mine.

It didn't have to be said. They both understood.

"I've getting ready to run into town for a few to pick up some things. I thought I'd see if you were up yet and wanted to go with me," Logan offered.

"I'd love to," Clara said. "Just give me a second to clean up the breakfast dishes."

"I've got this," Abby said. "You two go ahead."

"Are you sure?" Clara asked.

"Yes. You made it. It's only fair I clean up. Thanks for chatting with me," Abby said. "Logan, can you give us just a second?"

"Sure, I'll bring one of the four-wheelers around for us to take to where the cars are," Logan said. "Meet you out front." He sent a heated look toward Clara then patted Abby on the shoulder as he left them.

Abby reached into her pocket and pulled a card out then handed it to Clara. "This is my personal card."

"What do I need this for?"

"In case you find a guitar for Logan."

Clara shook her head. "I have my own money. If I find one, I'll grab it for him."

Abby nodded, and Clara knew the other woman understood. Clara wanted to give this gift to Logan on her own.

"Thanks for telling me," Clara said.

"I hope you find one," Abby replied.

Not giving herself a chance to second-guess her impulse, Clara reached out and hugged Abby before turning and heading out to join Logan.

"Everything good?" he asked, already seated and ready to go.

"Yes," Clara said, jumping on the four-wheeler behind him. She leaned into him, wrapping her arms around his waist and laying her head against his back as he pulled out and headed toward the area they kept the vehicles parked in. Everything was so organized here. It was nice. It was like being back home.

Thinking about that brought her Uncle Thomas to mind again. She was really worried about him. Not because he was gone, but because no one knew where he was. And Gideon had gone looking for him. Why? It still made no sense to her.

Logan parked the four-wheeler and hopped off. He helped her slide from the seat and pulled her into his arms.

"Worried about your uncle?" he asked, and she nodded. "We'll find him," he assured her.

She might not know he cooked or played guitar. But Logan knowing exactly what she was worried about… It was just the reminder she needed to remember the connection they did share.

It was a fun trip into town. It took some maneuvering on her part, but she got him to let her run a few errands on her own. She was just stowing the acoustic guitar she'd found at a second-hand shop in the car when he found her. She'd hurriedly threw one of the blankets that were kept in the car over it before he was close enough to see.

"Get everything you need?" he asked, trying to peek around her.

She smacked his arm playfully. "I got what I wanted. You finished?"

"One more stop," he said, reaching for her hand and tugging her with him. She turned to beep the car locked with the extra fob he'd given her. She didn't want anyone taking the present she'd picked out for him.

"Where are we going?" she asked, looking around.

"There's a shop on the end I want you to see. It's the whole reason I picked this particular shopping center."

When she saw the place he meant, she blushed. It was a lingerie and toy store.

"I believe you promised me new cuffs," he said, bending low so only she heard him.

"I did," she agreed.

She took her time in the store. It was weird but it seemed natural to be looking at toys and bondage gear with Logan, as if this wasn't their first time shopping for it. Logan picked something up and held it out to her.

"I like the looks of this," he said.

"What is it?" She turned the box in her hands and read it. It was a vibrator egg with a detached remote that the partner could use. "Only if they have one for you, too," she told him.

"Oh, baby, trust me, this is for me," he said and took it back, tucking it under his arm.

By the time they left, they'd filled two bags and were giggling like kids at Christmas. Logan was a kinky bastard, and he was hers, all hers. She was feeling young and carefree for the first time in forever as they walked toward the car. Then it hit her, and she came to a dead stop, eyes scanning everywhere, inhaling deeply through her nose.

"What is it?" Logan whispered, tensing beside her.

"I smell something," she whispered back. "And I feel like someone's watching us."

"Good or bad?" Logan asked. "I mean, I have trouble taking my eyes off you, as well, and I am pretty devastating when it comes to good looks."

Clara snorted, trying to hold back a laugh. She inhaled again, filtering through the mishmash of scents around them. She shook her head and started walking again. "The scent's not fresh enough, and there's too many others bleeding through for me to lock on it. Whoever it was, they've moved away." She glanced around, taking in the landscape around them. "Not too far, though. I definitely feel like they're watching us."

"Any ideas? Are we talking hunters?"

"I don't think so. I don't feel…hunted," she said then shook her head. "That sounds stupid."

"Baby, after all you've been through and what I've seen, I'd say hunted is a perfect way to describe it. We'll keep our eyes and ears open," Logan vowed.

They got in the Jeep, and Logan pulled his phone out while he was starting the car.

"Hey, got everything. We're heading back now. Clara felt some eyes on us, though." Logan glanced her way. "I'll let you talk to her. I'm going to take a bit of a longer route back, just to be on the safe side. Uh, huh. Yeah." He nodded his head. "Here she is." He held the phone out to her.

"Hello?"

"So what did you sense?" Reno's voice came over the line.

She glanced at Logan in question. She'd expected Tah to be on the other end of the line. She mouthed a question to her mate. *'Where's Tah?'*

"Labs with Finn and Murphy," Logan whispered. "Talk to Reno."

"Clara? You there?" Reno asked.

"Yes, sorry," she said. "I'm not sure. Logan and I were crossing the parking lot, and I could feel eyes on us. Could be nothing more than idle curiosity."

"You usually stop because someone is just being curious?"

"No," she admitted with a sigh.

"Then we take it seriously. Do you think anyone followed you when you trailed Amia and me back here?"

"No," she said as she thought back. "I didn't feel anyone on my tail."

"I didn't exactly feel you on mine, either," Reno reminded her.

"I've been a fully merged shifter since I was a child," Clara said. "No offense, Reno, but you're still learning."

"You're right." He surprised her by agreeing. "I'm thinking Tah and I could utilize you more with learning some of the ins and outs of our gifts. Well, you and Murphy and Zane."

"Murphy, huh?" she asked, sharing a look with Logan who she could tell was trying to make out both sides of the conversation based on her replies.

He nodded his head, letting her know he already knew about Murphy. So the shifters among them were starting to come forward. All except for one, it seemed.

"We have a lot to learn about using our senses and skills to their fullest potential," Reno said, bringing her back to the conversation.

"I'll do my best to help," Clara said.

"I'm sorry," Reno said into the silence that filled the airwaves after her comment.

She didn't need to ask what for.

"I saw Amia hurting, and I just couldn't focus on anything else."

"It's the way it is with mates," Clara said. "Her emotions are yours and vice versa."

"Still," Reno said. "I know how Amia was treated when we first arrived here. You were treated just as badly. I'm sorry for my role in it."

"Thank you, Reno. I appreciate it."

"Tell Logan to stop down at the lab as soon as he gets back. The Professor wants more blood."

"Everything okay?"

"Who knows? I'm putting nothing past him anymore. Tah will definitely keep a closer eye on what's going on down there."

"I can understand that," Clara said. "Reno?"

"Yeah?" he asked.

"We need to keep this absolutely quiet," she said, expressing her concerns out loud for the first time. "If anyone finds out what the Professor has created…" She let her voice trickle off. There were just no words to convey how much worse things could become at that point.

"Trust me, we're already aware of that," Reno admitted with a sigh.

"I just wanted to make sure," she said.

"Way ahead of you on this one," Reno said with a chuckle. "Tell Logan to watch his six. See you when you get back." And he hung up before she could reply.

Logan glanced at her and raised his shoulders. "Well?"

"He apologized to me."

"Good," Logan said, eyes back on the road. He'd driven in circles and was heading the opposite way of where they needed to go at the moment.

"He also asked me to help him and Tah learn more about shifting and using their senses."

"Makes sense," Logan said. "Probably have Zane and Murphy help out with that as well now that they've come forward as shifters."

"I'm guessing Zane's a panther like Orsai is. What about Murphy?"

"He's a Eurasian Lynx."

"Get out!" Clara exclaimed, sitting up with excitement. "Uncle Thomas thought they were all gone."

"From what I heard, Murphy said he's the last one," Logan told her. "Who's Orsai?"

"Remember the guy I told you about? The one who came around and taught us a bunch of stuff, like how blood transfusions helped during pregnancy?"

Logan nodded.

"That was Orsai. I figure he has to be related to Zane somehow. They look far too much alike not to be. I'm surprised Zane didn't know how to help Abby."

"Zane stays out of the house more often than not. He usually only comes in to cook when it's his turn or to grab a plate at mealtime. And to sleep, obviously. Otherwise, he seems to avoid the house."

Clara had an idea of why he was doing that, but she'd leave that to Zane. His business, not hers.

"So I hear you're some type of master chef in the kitchen," she purred.

He shot a glance her way again. "I like to cook," was all he said.

"I think a man who knows his way around a kitchen is sexy."

He grinned. "I think you like it better that I know my way around your pussy."

Her jaw dropped open, and she just looked at him for a minute in shock. He glanced at her again and wiggled his brows. She couldn't stop the giggle that spilled out.

"You're so bad," she admonished.

"You know it," he said with cockiness. "And you love it."

She nodded. She really did.

Chapter Twelve

It was later than Logan had planned when they got back, but he'd wanted to make sure no one was following them. They were planning a long-overdue celebration. He didn't want anything else to happen that might dampen it.

"Just leave the stuff here," Logan said when he opened Clara's door. "Someone will come get it."

She shook her head. "No way I'm leaving what we purchased for someone else to bring up."

He loved the way she blushed.

"I didn't take you for a prude," Logan said.

She grinned. "Hell, I have plans for those cuffs later, or at least one pair of them."

Now he was grinning. "Grab those bags, leave the rest."

She laughed as she rummaged and found what she wanted. She pulled a familiar looking case out and handed it to him.

"What's this?"

"Has it really been that long?

He gave her a funny look.

"It's a guitar, Logan. Tah said you used to play. I like music." She shrugged it off as if it was no big thing, but to him it was a lot.

"Thank you," he whispered, dropping a soft kiss on her lips.

"It was Abby's suggestion. I just happened to be the one going into town with you."

"And the one who picked it out and paid for it, I'm betting."

She nodded.

"Then thank you. I love to play. It's been a while, though."

"Are you as good with it as you are in the kitchen?"

He grinned. "It's a talent really." He leaned close and whispered, "How good I am with my hands."

She shivered, and he loved it. He could feel her desire as if it were a rope connecting them together.

"Finn's awake," Zane said, stepping out of the woods and spooking him.

"Jesus!" Logan said. "You scared ten years off my life."

"Good thing I'm on your side," Zane said. "Did you have a tail?"

"Not that I could see," Logan answered.

Clara shook her head, as well. "I didn't pick up on anything."

"I'll keep my eyes peeled anyway," Zane said. "I'll hang out here for a bit just to be on the safe side. Send one of the others back if there's anything perishable in here. Otherwise, I'll get it when I head back."

"Nothing this trip," Logan assured him. "It can wait until you head in."

"See you there," Zane said and turned to merge into the trees once more.

"You didn't know he was there?" Logan asked her.

She shrugged. "I did. I just didn't think about it. It was Zane."

"How did you know?"

"He has a unique scent he gives off, a pheromone. We all do. Mates' scents tend to merge and they both carry it."

"I don't smell anything."

"You won't. You'll have an enhanced sense of smell above human standards, but it won't match mine. When taught how to sort through smells, a shifter can always tell when another shifter is around. Unless they have the ability to block their scent."

"Is that possible?" Logan asked.

"Anything is possible," Clara said with a shrug. "I'm proof of that."

Logan thought about that on the way back to the house on the four-wheeler. It was that or give in to the boner throbbing in his pants from Clara wrapped so tightly against his back. Her nipples pressed into him and he could feel the heat of her pussy. He wanted to take her to their room, strip her naked and have a night similar to the one before. But he needed to go check in with Tah, and he'd like to see how Finn was doing now that he was awake.

"Why don't you take the bags up to our room while I check in with Tah real quick?" Logan suggested. "Then meet me back down here, and we'll go to the labs together."

"Sounds good," she replied and reached up to pull his head down to hers.

She kissed him, using that tongue of hers in a way that reminded him of how it felt wrapped around his dick. Damn, he was going to be bursting his jeans at this rate. He groaned as she stepped back and watched as her gaze fell to his crotch. He shook his head when she grinned at him.

"You little vixen," he muttered.

She knew exactly what she was doing to him.

"Just wanted to make sure you saved some time for me later," she replied and turned away, squatting to pick up the bags and guitar she'd set down before kissing him.

He swatted her on the ass when she stood up and moved to head for the stairs. She threw a sultry look over her shoulder and put an extra wiggle in her walk.

"Damn," he muttered under his breath and heard her laugh. He shook his head, adjusted his dick and went in search of Tah. He found Tah and Reno in the office.

"Anyone tailing you?" Tah asked as Logan stepped in.

"Not that either one of us saw," Logan said. "Clara never picked up on it again. What did I miss? Zane said Finn's awake?"

"Awake and moving," Tah grunted. "Whatever is in that shit the Professor concocted is powerful. It's like looking at someone who was never injured."

"His face? The bruises? Swelling?" Logan asked.

"Gone. All gone," Reno said. "The plan was to operate as soon as he was stable enough. Diane said within a few hours he was fine. Hell, you wouldn't even know he'd been stabbed except for the scar on his stomach. Whatever the Professor's been working on is some serious shit. We don't even heal that quickly."

"Wow." Logan whistled. "That's a little scary."

"You don't know the half of it," Tah said.

"Well?" Logan prompted.

"We were hoping to find out what happened from Finn. Find out who took him. We suspect hunters, but was it the Blanes or someone else? We were hoping to see if he remembered who came in and killed the guys holding him."

"He looked pretty bad. Maybe he wasn't conscious?" Logan suggested.

"Who knows?" Tah said, then dropped a bomb. "He has no memory."

"What?" Logan asked.

"Last thing he remembers is getting Reno's message and heading here to find us. Nothing since," Tah said.

"Jesus," Logan uttered. "That's months lost. Is it from the shot?"

"The Professor isn't sure. At this point, we don't know if he'll remember eventually or forget more," Tah said. "The Professor's running more tests," he added with disgust.

"Whatever the outcome, Finn's alive, Tah," Logan said. "That counts for something. Besides, have you thought that maybe it has little to do with what the Professor gave him and more to do with his mind protecting him? You saw what they did to him. Hell, would you want to remember how you got like that?"

Tah sighed and rubbed the back of his neck. He seemed to be doing that a lot lately. "I don't know," he admitted. "I was hoping for answers. It would help if we knew if it was the Blanes who took him or not."

"Zane said he took pictures. Have Amia look." Logan glanced at Reno. "She's seen worse, I'm sure, and if it's the Blanes, she might recognize someone."

Tah looked toward Reno.

"Yeah," Reno agreed. "She might be able to. I'll have Zane show them to us."

There was a time when Logan would have teased Reno about the 'us', asking if Amia was allowed to do anything without Reno. But now that Logan was mated, he understood.

"Anything else?" he asked.

Reno shook his head. "So far it's just the memory."

"He's already demanding to get out of the labs and help out," Tah stated. "I think he might be worse than you as a patient as far as Diane is concerned."

Logan laughed. "I was pretty rotten to her."

"Knock, knock," Clara said, pausing at the door. "Am I interrupting?"

"No," Tah waved her in. "I wanted to see you, get your take on what you felt when you and Logan were in town. Where were you when it happened?"

Logan shared a glance with Clara, taking in her big eyes and understanding she was not down with telling Tah and Reno they had gone to the toy store. Of course just remembering all they'd picked up had his dick perking up again.

"We went to the North Plaza," Logan said. "It was the closest place that had all we wanted to pick up."

"That's on the edge of town," Tah said. "There's a touch of woods to the left of the parking lot. Anyone could have been hiding and watching."

"I didn't feel a sense of danger," Clara said. "I don't know if that makes sense or not. It wasn't like I felt threatened really or anything along those lines. It was just a knowing that someone was watching us."

"I understand that," Reno said. "I felt the same way when you were in the woods with Amia and me. I knew you were there, but didn't feel a sense that you were there to do harm."

"Exactly," Clara said, then narrowed her eyes. "You think it was another shifter?"

"Makes sense," Reno said, glancing at Tah.

"Wait," Logan interjected. "Wouldn't you have caught a scent, like you did with Zane?"

"You can scent other shifters?" Tah asked.

Clara nodded. "You can, too. All you have to do is know how to sort through the scents around you. It's like being able to scent danger or lust or fear when you're around other people."

"Is it something you can teach us to do?" Reno asked.

She looked thoughtful for a moment then slowly nodded. "I can try. Honestly, it's not hard once you get a feel for it. You'll pick it up quickly. I'm betting you've already started picking up on it a bit."

"Maybe," Tah said. "But it would be nice to recognize what it is I'm picking up on."

"It's easier to learn certain things when you're shifted. Your animal instincts are stronger, and you'll just know what to do. Then you learn to bring that out when you're in this form. It's about learning perfect balance, learning how to enhance without doing a full shift." She flicked her hands out in front of her and the claws of her lioness appeared. "Handy when I need them but don't have time for a full shift."

"Your eyes are glowing that sexy yellow again," Logan murmured.

She also had a stripe of darker brown across her face this time, like a mask.

"All you need is a cape," he said.

She laughed. He loved the sound of her laugh.

"My senses are on par with the animal at the moment. So a bit of it comes through, but just a bit. I'm in full control, a merged control. Not one or the other, but both."

"So first we learn to do a full shift and then we learn to do a partial?" Reno grunted. "Jesus, this shit is complicated."

"You have no idea," Clara muttered. "But if it was a shifter watching us, they were too far away when I picked up on it. I scented something, but it wasn't fresh and was too diluted with other scents for me to get a lock on it."

"Do you think your uncle might be searching for you here?" Tah asked.

Clara shrugged. "I don't know. I'd like to be able to get in touch with him or Gideon, just to find out exactly what's going on."

"Is Lydia a threat?" Tah asked and Logan saw Reno tense at the mention of Amia's mother.

"I don't know," Clara admitted. "There was a time when I would have given you an immediate no. But now? I'm just not sure. She's so filled with hate and a need for revenge. It's polluted her mind to everything else."

"Sounds like a threat to me," Reno said.

Clara sighed. "It's not a simple question, Reno. No matter what you think. I can't look at her without seeing the woman who tried to save my father, the woman my father sent to us. And I get what you're seeing, as well—the woman who abandoned her daughter to a group of people like the Blanes. But just for one minute, imagine a woman knowing she was going to die. She escaped but had to leave her daughter behind. Not by choice, but because there was no way to get to her and take her along. Imagine living with that guilt. I'm not making excuses for Lydia. I'm just trying to show you another side. Nothing is black and white. No one is pure evil or pure good. We all have a darkness to us."

Reno said nothing, but Logan knew Clara had given his friend something to think about.

"The Professor wanted to see us down in the lab again," Logan said.

Tah nodded, then dropped his head forward and rubbed the bridge of his nose with his fingers. Logan wished there was a way to take the burden of everything off Tah's shoulders. Even when they'd been in the Marines together, Tah had been the one stepping up and taking charge, taking responsibility for everyone on himself. He was still doing it.

"He looks so stressed, like the weight of the world is on his shoulders," Clara whispered as they left the room and headed down the hall.

"He is," Logan agreed.

"He isn't alone in this. He shouldn't have the burden of everything on himself. He needs a council or something. That way there's a group of people in charge so they all share the burden."

Logan stopped and pulled her to him for a quick kiss. "That's a brilliant idea. I'll bring it up to him when we're done in the labs."

"More blood?" Clara asked with a groan. "How much does the Professor need?"

Logan snickered. "You have no idea. Any time he sees you he'll ask for more blood. Of course, now we know what he's been doing with some of it."

"You have to admit it's really brilliant, what he came up with. Scary, but brilliant."

"In theory, yes. From what I just heard, scary is winning out over brilliant at the moment. Finn's completely healed, as in doesn't even look like he was injured at all."

"Holy shit!' Clara exclaimed.

"Yeah," Logan nodded. "Now we have to wait and see how Finn reacts in the aftermath to what he was given. As it is, he has no memory of what happened. Last thing he remembers is heading here."

"Really?" Clara asked. "That seems like an odd reaction."

Logan shrugged as they stepped into the lab. "Who knows? You saw what—" He broke off as he took in Finn standing before him. "Holy fuck! You look…"

"Like nothing happened to me?" Finn asked. "Yeah, I've been getting that a lot. Just wish I could remember what the hell did happen to me. Murphy isn't saying much except I was at death's door and the Professor saved me with some shot that might grant me superpowers."

Logan's lips twitched at that, but Clara burst into laughter.

"That's one way to look at it," she replied.

"Well, hello, gorgeous," Finn said, smiling a little too much for Logan's liking.

A growl sounded in the air, and both Clara and Finn turned to look at Logan with surprise. Shit! Was he growling? From the broad grin on his mate's face, it was definitely coming from him. She cuddled into him, rubbing her face against his chest. He felt it expand with pride. Jesus! You'd think he was the one with a beast inside.

"So that's the way of it, huh?" Finn asked, but he didn't seem disappointed. In fact, he immediately turned to Diane when she walked in. "Hello, gorgeous."

Diane sighed. Clara giggled again, and Logan shook his head.

"God save me," Diane muttered before turning on Finn. "I told you not to just wander around down here. This isn't a playground."

Finn began fingering some paperwork on the counter.

Diane slapped his hand. "And for God's sake, don't touch anything."

"We're here to give more blood," Clara said. "Should we find the Professor?"

"No, I'll take care of it. He's been in his office all morning and hasn't come out," Diane informed them, turning to pull the supplies she needed out of the drawers in front of her.

"Everything okay?" Logan asked.

Diane turned back to them with a smile pasted on her face, but Logan could see right through it. Something had the doctor shaken.

"You just missed Abby," she said. "That little guy of hers is more active than I've seen him in a long time." She glanced at Clara as she prepped Logan's arm. "Any ideas on when I'll need to give her another pint of Tah's blood?"

Clara shrugged. "You'll just have to watch her. When you see the signs of fatigue setting in again, give her more."

Diane nodded as she pulled the needle out of Logan's arm. She'd filled four vials this time. She immediately turned to Clara, tossing the used needle and grabbing a fresh one before grabbing four more vials and setting them out to be filled.

"So I heard we might have some kind of celebration?" Diane asked as she worked.

"Logan's planning it," Clara said with a smile that shot straight to Logan's heart.

"Just a day of fun for a change," Logan said.

"A whole day?" Diane looked surprised.

"Sometimes it's important to remember what we're doing everything for," Logan reminded her then glanced at Clara. "And who."

"It sounds wonderful to me," Diane said, finishing with Clara and cleaning up. "So what are you two up to for the rest of the night?"

Logan glanced at Clara and swore sparks charged the air between them.

"Looks like something a lot more interesting than anything you or I have planned," Finn said with a chuckle.

Diane smiled, but Logan could see sadness in her eyes. "I'm really happy for you two."

"Thank you," Clara said, and Logan gave Diane a one-armed hug.

"You better watch out, Nurse Ratchet. This mating thing seems to be spreading. Who knows who'll be the next one bitten by it!"

Clara snorted, and Finn laughed. But Diane's eyes got a little wide before she turned with a wave of her hand and buried her nose in the paperwork on the counter. She didn't say anything and Logan understood they'd been dismissed from the labs. He took Clara's hand again and gave Finn a wave before heading upstairs once more.

"Finn seem okay to you?" Logan asked her.

Clara shrugged. "I don't really know him, but he seemed pretty happy-go-lucky to me. Doesn't seem stressed about not remembering."

"But did you scent anything on him?"

She was just opening her mouth to reply when the alarm went off.

"Fuck!" Logan yelled and took off at a run with Clara on his heels. "Someone triggered a sensor."

He burst out the door at the top and saw Abby getting ready to head down to the labs where she was supposed to stay with Diane. It was a safety measure to make sure Abby and the baby were as protected as possible. No one wanted another episode like what she'd been through with Harlan Jones. The labs were reinforced and had a room where Abby could be locked in and kept safe.

"Tell Finn to stay with you," Logan yelled to Abby. "Tell him Tah wants him as your personal guard."

"Already planned to," Abby said, squeezing his shoulder then Clara's hand as they passed. "Stay safe. Keep him safe for me."

"We will," Clara answered for them. Logan knew his mate understood Abby was talking about Tah.

Logan saw Holt stepping out of the control room. Kenzie was inside, watching the screens. "Who's on patrol?" he asked.

"Reno, Amia and Vic have been on night-shift this week," Holt answered, joining them in a jog toward the front door.

"Where's everyone else?" Logan demanded.

"Haven't seen Zane," Holt answered. "Tah headed out to find Reno. Fuck, we need a better way to communicate then with these phones. We need military-grade headsets."

"You find me a way to get them, and I'll do it." Logan grunted back. "We're doing the best we can with what we have. And our funds are seriously limited at the moment. "

Holt nodded. "Sorry."

They were only at the edge of the woods when Clara stopped and lifted her nose to the air, inhaling deeply.

"What is it?" Logan asked.

"Fuck!" Clara exploded as she started stripping her shoes and clothes off. "That's Lydia." Her eyes were glowing when she met his again. "And she's not alone."

The next thing Logan saw was a lioness leaping through the air. She turned back and looked at him once with Clara's golden-brown eyes, then she disappeared among the trees. He took off after her with Holt on his heels. The other man had gotten a good look at Logan's mate, but it wasn't jealousy that beat in Logan's chest. It was pride. And one word filled his mind. Beautiful. Clara as a lioness was even more breathtaking than he'd imagined.

Chapter Thirteen

Clara hated leaving Logan behind, but she couldn't shake the feeling that something was wrong. She'd learned to trust her instincts. If Lydia was here it wasn't to play catch-up with Amia. And who knew what she'd told whomever she'd brought with her, because the one thing Clara was certain of was that Lydia wouldn't have come alone. The problem was Clara couldn't seem to focus on any scent other than Lydia's at the moment. Whatever was about to happen, she knew Lydia was the center of it.

She kept running, letting the scent filling her nose guide her in the right direction. Suddenly the trees cleared out a bit and she saw Reno and Amia standing there. Another woman lay slumped on the ground a few feet from them. Clara guessed it was Vic, and she wasn't moving. Please, God, don't let them have killed her.

Reno was trying to stand in front of Amia, but she was having none of it. And in front of them with gun drawn was Lydia with a shifter Clara knew far too well standing behind her. Clara should have guessed. Dillion. If there was anyone as bitter as Lydia, it was Dillion whose entire family had been wiped out by hunters. Dillion carried a thirst for vengeance that had to rival Lydia's. Clara should have seen an alliance like theirs coming.

"Move out of the way," Lydia was screaming. "I don't want to hurt you. I have to kill her. She's evil. Blane blood is running through her veins."

"Wrong," Amia yelled back. "I left them just like you did. Only I didn't turn my back on what they did. I kept doing my all to rescue people. What did you do? Hide like the coward you are!"

"No," Lydia said, shaking her head back and forth as if confused.

"She's evil," Dillion yelled. "A Blane. A Hunter."

"You're evil," Lydia said again. "Evil."

Clara understood what Lydia was doing even if no one else did. It wasn't about telling Amia she was bad or evil or whatever. It was about blocking out the guilt of leaving Amia behind. Why could no one else see that? And why was Dillion feeding it?

"Listen, bitch," Amia said and shoved in front of Reno.

Lydia lifted the gun.

Clara took it all in as she closed the distance between them. Faster, she needed to be faster. Reno took Amia to the ground. Tah burst through the trees opposite of her with a roar that had even her wanting to stop and fall to her knees. But she took the leap needed to put her where she wanted to be. Lydia fired the gun. Clara felt a burn along her back flank and landed in a heap on the ground.

"No!" Lydia screamed.

Clara tried to turn toward the other woman but her leg collapsed underneath her. She could feel her animal whimpering in pain as the shift began. What the fuck had been in that bullet? Her leg felt as if it was on fire.

She blinked her eyes several times, taking a few seconds like always to adjust from seeing out of her cat's eyes back to her human eyes.

"No," she tried to yell, but it came out weakly.

Tah had Lydia dangling in the air, one hand wrapped around her throat. Reno had Dillion on the ground, knee to his back and both hands jerked up toward his shoulder blades. Amia was crawling toward Clara.

"Clara!" Logan's voice filled the clearing, and she struggled to turn her head toward him.

"Clara," Amia said, touching her leg.

Clara screamed in agony as another wave of fire shot through her.

"Jesus!" Amia breathed. "What the fuck is that?"

"Logan," Clara moaned as she felt him drop down beside her. Her vision started to blur.

"I'm here. I got you, baby," he said next to her ear.

"Don't let them be harmed." She struggled to get the words out. "Need answers. Need them."

She didn't hear his answer, didn't even know if he'd heard her. Everything went black as she was sucked under.

Logan thought about grabbing Clara and running, but she needed to reach the house quicker than he'd be able to move. If he were a shifter, it would be different. He'd seen how much faster the shifters were even in human form. He glanced around the clearing.

"Reno," he called. "I need you. Now."

Reno was there beside him in an instant. "Get her to the house, to Diane. I don't know what she was shot with, but it's knocked her the fuck out. Jesus! Go fast, Reno. Get her there as quickly as you can."

Reno clapped him on the shoulder, scooped Clara up and took off. Logan didn't even care that his mate was naked. He only cared that she made it back to those who could help her in time.

"Tah." He turned quickly to intercede. "We need her."

"I know," Tah roared and shook Lydia again." What did you shoot her with? What?"

She gurgled but obviously couldn't answer.

"It's what we call a sludge bullet," the guy on the ground answered. His eyes were on Tah, but not with awe. It was more of a calculated look as if he was plotting something and was just waiting for the opportune moment.

"What's that?" Logan demanded.

"When it pierces the skin the liquid inside starts seeping free and releasing into the blood stream."

"What is it?" Logan screamed, grabbing the guy and shaking him. He thought he felt a prick on the back of his hand but ignored it.

The guy bared his canines at Logan but jerked back as Tah growled low in his throat. Even Logan could hear the threat in Tah's growl.

"I don't know," the guy said. "I swear! I don't know. Lydia made it."

Logan wasn't sure he believed him. "If anything happens to my mate, I'll rip your fucking head off," Logan warned and stood up. "I'm heading to the house. I've got to check on Clara."

Tah nodded. "We've got this."

Amia had moved over to where Vic was laying. Tah held Lydia still, though now she stood on the ground in front of him. Holt had the shifter she'd brought with her face down on the ground, arms wide of his body. Murphy burst out of the clearing with Zane. Logan left them to it and ran full out toward the house. Holt was right. They needed a better form of communication. He really wanted to know how his mate was doing.

He prayed while he ran, something he hadn't done in a long time. He might not go to church, but he had faith. The last few months had shown him just how strong his faith was.

"Please, God, if you're up there watching us. Please don't take Clara from me. I just found her." He spoke aloud as he ran, repeating the words over again and again. "Pleased don't take her from me."

He hit the front porch and slammed into the house, taking the stairs down to the lab in leaps.

"Oh, fuck no!" he yelled, coming around the corner and seeing Clara laying too still on one of the tables. Her eyes were closed, one arm hanging limply off the table beside her. Someone had thrown a sheet over her body, hiding her nudity. He needed to touch her. His heart felt as if it was going to burst from his chest and a surge of anger fired through him.

"Logan!"

He could hear Diane's voice but all of his focus was on his mate and getting to her.

"Logan!"

Finn stepped in front of him, and Logan shoved him out of the way.

The Professor hollered something. Diane moved. Logan finally reached Clara.

"Logan." The Professor was in his face.

"I'm taking blood. I need your arm now."

"Not now," Logan grunted, eyes focused on Clara. He reached for her fingers and twined his through them.

"Now, Logan," the Professor ordered.

"Not fucking now!" Logan roared.

"Logan." Diane shoved her face in front of his, demanding his attention. "She's fine. Clara's fine. The bullet contained a sedative. That's it. It might have burned as it hit her bloodstream, but she's okay. Just sleeping. The wound is already healing."

"She's sleeping?" he asked.

"Yes," Clara said. "Give the Professor your arm."

Logan held his arm out and felt the needle pierce his skin. "Why do you need blood now?"

She gave him a strange look. "Your eyes, Logan," Diane said. "They're glowing. Your eyes are glowing like your mate's do."

"Well, fuck," Logan said. "What does that mean?"

"No idea," the Professor said as he worked on filling another vial with blood. "But we'll figure it out."

"Where's Reno?" Logan asked. He could feel his heart rate finally slowing down. He hadn't realized how wound up he was.

"He took Abby back upstairs. We weren't sure at first what kind of liquid was in the bullet Clara took. I wanted Abby out of here just in case," Diane said. She had her fingers on the wrist of the hand he had twined with Clara. "Good. Take a few deep breaths for me. Pulse is slowing down." She glanced at him, meeting and holding his gaze. "What happened, Logan? What got you so revved up?"

Logan shrugged. "Clara and I heard the alarms when we were heading upstairs. We met Holt and all three of us headed out together. Clara shifted and took off ahead of us. Holt and I followed as quickly as we could. I heard the shot."

"Deep breath," Diane said. "Pulse is picking up again. Remember, Clara's fine. She's just sleeping."

"Sleeping," Logan murmured. "I heard the shot and tried to run faster. When we got to the clearing where everyone was, I saw Tah holding who I'm guessing is Lydia Blane in the air by her neck. There was another shifter on the ground. Reno had him. And Amia was by Clara. She was sprawled out and there was blood all over her leg."

He saw Diane throw a glance to the Professor.

"Logan, I need you to calm down. Whatever is running through your head, you need to clear it out," the Professor said.

"I'm fine," Logan said. "I'm calm." His glance fell to Clara again. "She's just sleeping?"

"Clara's only sleeping, Logan. Give me your hand. Let go of her for a minute and give me your hand," Diane said, tugging at his fingers.

"No," Logan said. He needed to touch is mate. Needed it. Felt as if he might die without it.

"Logan, did you get hit with anything?" Diane asked. "Finn, get a hold of someone now. Call all their phones until someone answers."

Logan felt her turn back to him.

"There's a mark on the back of your hand. It's a little swollen and red. It looks almost like a bug bite or an injection site."

She finally tugged his hand free and Logan felt cold, so cold. Diane was asking him something, but he couldn't focus.

"What happened, Logan?" Diane yelled.

"Not the sedative," the Professor interjected. "Logan, stay with us, boy. Stay with us."

But he couldn't. He could feel himself slipping away in his mind. "Shifter…did something…"

"Logan!" Diane yelled. "Don't you dare fucking pass out on me!"

"I'm here," he whispered, shaking his head. "Where's Clara?"

"Right here."

Diane put his hand back on Clara's. He took it like a lifeline.

"What's going on?" Tah burst in the room with Abby. "Finn called and said Logan was injured."

"Professor!" Diane called. "He's burning up."

"Cold," Logan challenged her. He wasn't hot at all. He was freezing.

"What the hell happened? He was fine when he left the clearing," Tah roared.

"Well all that bellowing isn't going to help anything," the Professor fired back.

"Logan, what happened to you?" Abby's touch was hot against his skin and he groaned, pulling away from her.

"Shifter…" Logan tried to say again. His mouth felt funny, like his words were getting all garbled up.

"Was there another shifter there?" the Professor asked.

"Lydia brought a shifter with her. He said his name is Dillion," Tah answered.

"Where is he? Who's with him?" Diane asked frantically.

"Zane has him. They're putting them both in rooms downstairs until we figure out what the hell to do," Tah said.

"Oh, God, no," Diane moaned, turning on him with huge eyes. "We think he injected Logan with something. Not sure what, but it seems to be bringing some major changes out in him."

"What changes?" Tah demanded.

"He was shaking with rage when he got here. His pulse was frantic, breathing labored and not just from the run to get here. His eyes glowed, Tah," Diane said. "Imagine if whatever he was given was injected in a shifter. Logan is human."

"Fuck!" Tah groaned, pulling out his phone.

"We could have a real mess on our hands here. I need that shifter down here so I can see what he gave Logan. He'll have to have it on him somewhere," the Professor said.

"Reno," Tah spoke into the phone. "Tell Zane to watch out for Dillion. The kid's got something on him. Looks like he hit Logan with it. Don't trust him." Tah paused and they all heard a loud growl followed by the sound of jaws snapping together and then a long hiss. "What the fuck was that?"

"Ahh, fuck!" Reno's yell came through the phone. "Zane. Fuck! Zane!"

There was the sound of the phone being jostled then hitting the floor. A scuffle followed by another one of those growls, snaps and hiss sounds, then nothing. Logan heard it all as if it were happening in the room next to him. It made no sense. Were his senses that enhanced just from mating with Clara?

"What's going on?" he mumbled. He was suddenly feeling the heat Diane claimed his body was putting off and he was anything but tired. He stripped his shirt off over his head. "Hot. So hot."

All eyes shifted back to him, but it was different. They looked different. His vision was seriously fucked up. He shook his head, trying to clear it, but it didn't work.

"See," Diane said.

"Jesus Christ," Tah grunted. "His eyes are fucking glowing."

Holt burst into the room. "Little prick had this on him." He held a needle out to Diane. He said he gave lover boy some," Holt said, nodding toward Logan. "Then hit Zane with the rest of it."

"What happened down there?" Diane demanded.

"Holy shit," Holt said. "I've never seen anything like it. When he hit Zane with it, Zane reacted immediately. He threw the kid against the wall and went down in a crouch. He did this growl and snapped his teeth together. His eyes were fucked up, glowing and stuff. Then he hissed and it scared the shit out of me. Next thing we knew, he was bursting out of his clothes and taking off. Reno went after him."

"Did Dillion say anything about what it was?" Tah demanded.

"He said he hoped we enjoyed this taste of feral cat fever," Holt said.

"Oh, my God!" Diane moaned and turned huge eyes to Logan.

"What is it?" Abby demanded. "What does it do?"

"In Logan? I have no idea. Humans don't get feral cat fever. I'm guessing this is something they've cooked up. So I have no idea of the potency of it. There might be some traces left in the syringe. I'll run tests, but it'll take time."

Logan heard the catch in her voice before she continued.

"It's Zane I'm worried about. He's a full shifter."

"What will it do to him?" Tah asked.

"He's shifted into his panther. The fever will only strike faster now. He'll be like a primitive cat, Tah. Vicious, primal, deadly. He could kill someone. The fever will ravage his mind first shutting down his ability to reason, to think outside the animal at all. He'll essentially be no more than a lethal predator. God help anything or anyone that gets in his way," Diane told them.

"How long?" Tah asked.

"I don't know," Diane said. "I have no idea what exactly this Dillion gave them. I don't know how long it will affect Logan or Zane or what the repercussions of it will be. I just don't know."

"Why would a shifter have something like that?" Logan asked, shaking his head again as things came back into focus.

"To turn us against one another," Clara said.

Logan surged toward the table she lay on and leaned over her, lifting her up against his chest and hugging her close. "Baby, are you okay?"

"Groggy. My head is killing me. From what I just woke up to, it sounds like you're the one I should be worried about."

"I'll be fine," Logan tried to assure her. He rubbed his hands down her arms then over her shoulders. He groaned and rubbed over her again.

"What's that smell?" Tah asked, his nose scrunched up as if he didn't find it pleasant.

"I think you guys need to leave," Clara said softly, shifting on the table so she could sit up.

Logan helped her turn toward him, holding the sheet up so no one else would see Clara's perfect body. A growl rumbled through the room and Logan turned to glare at Tah. His friend had no reason to be making a sound like that right now.

"Did he just growl at me?" Tah asked, and it took Logan a minute to realize Tah was referring to him.

"You need to leave now," Clara said again, grasping Logan by the shoulders and pulling him close. "I think I might know what they gave him, or at least where it originated from."

"What is it?" the Professor and Diane both demanded at the same time.

"I'll tell you later," Clara said.

Logan felt his chest vibrate and that rumble filled the air again. He leaned closer into Clara, leaning low to nuzzle her neck, licking and nipping at the strong column.

"Leave. Now. Or you're going to get a show you don't want to see."

"What's going on, Clara?" Abby asked.

"That smell. The growl and glowing eyes. Logan's not just going primal. He's putting off some serious pheromones. I'd guess he's entering a sexual frenzy, and as his mate, I'm not far behind."

"Oh, shit," Diane said. "Any ideas how long this might last?"

"He's human. It should burn out of his system within twenty-four hours or less. But I'm only guessing. I've never seen a human hit with feral fever."

"Will you be okay?" Tah asked and Logan felt the rumble again.

"I'll be fine. I'm his mate. No matter what he wants from me, he'll never hurt me," Clara said. "Now go. And Tah..."

Logan heard his buddy stop.

"Yeah?"

"Don't go after Zane. You can't reach him right now. You'll only risk getting more of you hurt."

Logan heard the sigh, felt the beat of fear palpitating from someone, then heard nothing, felt nothing but Clara.

He pulled back and glanced around, noting he and Clara were all alone. He jerked the sheet from her with one hand and buried the other in her hair, pulling her head back and meeting her gaze. No fear. Only love, acceptance. His chest vibrated again as he leaned in close.

"Mine," he challenged her, some part of him waiting to see if she'd deny him.

"Yours," she agreed. "I'm all yours."

Chapter Fourteen

Logan took her mouth in a kiss meant to demonstrate who was in control. Clara knew he would never hurt her. She also knew he wasn't the same Logan right now. She'd purposely kept that from the others. Right now, Logan was pure alpha male, and his primal needs were controlling him—at the moment his desire for sex. Probably because they had recently mated and sex was often on both their minds. They were lucky it hadn't brought out rage or some other savage emotion in him. She'd seen it happen.

Logan scraped his teeth over her bottom lip and nipped it hard enough to draw a drop of blood.

"Mine," he told her again.

Damn, it was a little embarrassing to admit how much this Logan was turning her on. She really liked him all dominant and possessive. Not that he wasn't normally, but not quite on this level.

"So show me," Clara purred at him and scraped her nails down his chest, leaving grooves as she made her way to the button of his jeans.

He growled again, and she wondered if he got as turned on by the sound when she made it. Her pussy was beyond wet and ready for him. She shivered with anticipation when he pushed her hand away and ripped open his jeans, shoving them and his boxer briefs down to his knees before jerking her closer to the edge of the table.

He didn't waste any time in doing as she said and showing her. He pressed his cock against her and thrust deep.

"Mine," he rumbled once more as he pounded in and out of her.

Clara clawed at his shoulders, legs wrapped at his waist, as she held on. He was fucking her so hard the table was actually shaking, and she was enjoying every moment of it. There was no holding back for either of them. His heat became hers.

"That's it," she crooned. "Fuck me so good. Show me who I belong to."

He reached down and slid his hands under her knees, flipping her back on the table as he lifted her hips higher. She flung her hands out to catch her weight as she fell and let her head drop between her shoulders in ecstasy as he continued pounding.

"Oh, God! Yes! Yes!" she screamed as her orgasm rocked through her core and had tremors spiraling through her.

Logan just grunted and kept fucking as her juices soaked his cock. His hands were firm on the side edges of the table and he showed no sign of being anywhere close to coming with her.

"More," he uttered and shifted her legs until she was lying on her side on the table with her knees bent up toward her chest.

"Oh, God!" she yelled as he thrust deep. The angle in this position was unbelievable, and she was revving up toward another orgasm quickly.

"My pussy," he told her.

"My cock," she fired back.

He did that rumble and pumped his cock in and out a little faster. His grip was firm on her hip, but he slid the other hand up to fondle her nipples, pinching and tugging on them. Clara tried to turn her upper body into his touch, wanting to give him more access, or at least access to both breasts. He shoved his cock deep and bent down to suckle her nipple.

She wrapped one hand around his neck and held him to her while he sucked, licked and nibbled on her. He felt so good she couldn't stop her body from rocking on his cock. He lifted his head and shifted again, pulling his cock from her.

"No," she groaned in denial, wanting him back inside her, but Logan obviously had something else in mind.

He flipped her onto her back and came over her, pressing her flat to the table while he kissed her breathless. Slowly, he eased their mouths apart and trailed down her body with his lips. He nuzzled her, licked her and occasionally grazed or nipped her with his teeth. No part of her was left untouched, even her arms and legs were worshipped. She almost jumped when he sucked her big toe into his mouth, but those strong hands of his held her still for his bidding.

He kissed his way back up her inner thigh until he reached her pussy.

"Mine," he said against her skin and bit down on the inside of her thigh hard enough to mark her.

Clara cried out and jerked against his hold. Not in fear or pain, but in sensual delight at the way he claimed her. It called to the lioness within her. He flicked his gaze up to meet hers and she saw desire still burning in his eyes. If that look was anything to go by, she was going to have a long fulfilling night.

He slid his tongue between her pussy lips and ran it up to her clit. He licked over the taut bud then flicked it, stabbing at it with his tongue. She tried to lift her hips again, but he held her in place.

"Mine." He grunted, raising his head a bit as he met her gaze again.

She reached down and sank the fingers of both hands into his hair, jerking his head back down to her pussy. He nipped her in a display of dominance, a reminder from him that he was in charge. Then he dropped to her pussy with a groan and began pumping his tongue in and out of her, lapping up her juices.

"Yesss," she hissed between her teeth as he slid his thumb up to rub over her clit.

Just that quickly she was coming again. Logan took in her orgasm and gave her another. She was panting for breath, her body one tremble after another as she drowned in pleasure when he finally moved back. She glanced at him with eyes half open and took in the rock-hard cock that stood out from his body. The head was flushed with pre-cum glistening on it. And suddenly she had her breath back and knew just what she wanted.

She licked her lips and watched his cock bounce as he moved around the table. She rolled over on her stomach and came up on her elbows watching as he stepped in front of her. One hand circled his cock, slowly pumping up and down his shaft. He rubbed his thumb over the head, smearing the pre-cum and making her mouth water.

She glanced up at him from beneath her lashes and opened wide. He took the invitation and pressed his cock into her mouth. She wrapped her lips around the crown and sucked greedily. He groaned in pleasure and dropped his hands to the edge of the table.

"Suck it," he commanded, but she was way ahead of him.

She wrapped one hand around it and dropped the forearm of her other arm down to provide more balance than just her elbow. She took as much of him as she could, loving the feel of the tip hitting the back of her throat. She swirled her tongue around him, circling the head and shaft as she worked his cock in and out. Every once in a while she would let him feel just a hint of teeth, mostly because she saw how much he liked it.

She was really getting into it, getting greedy to taste his cum on her tongue when he gripped her hair and gently pulled her off his cock.

"No," she groaned, coming up to her knees and grasping his shoulders with her hands. "I want to taste you."

He shook his head. "Fuck."

"Oh, yeah," she agreed.

Then he surprised her. He lifted her up and held her there while she squealed and wrapped her legs quickly around his waist. He lowered her onto his cock and just held her against him for a long moment while they both looked at each other.

"Mine," he whispered. "All mine."

"Mine." She gave him the words back. "All mine."

He took her by the waist and began lifting and lowering her on his dick. She gripped his shoulders and used them to allow her to aid him. It felt so good. Gravity was working with them, allowing her to take him impossibly deep every time she sank down on his shaft. She used her thighs to help her lift and lower. She was close to coming again. Her nipples brushing his chest with every movement and adding more stimulation.

"Oh, God," she cried. "I'm coming. I'm coming!"

He turned her then, as if that was what he'd been waiting for. Her back met the wall and her chest was flattened by Logan's. He powered into her, grunting and moaning with every thrust, riding her through her orgasm and sending her flying high into another one.

"Logan!"

She screamed his name as his cock jerked inside her. A hot pulse of cum filled her, then another as Logan fucked her mercilessly. She leaned forward and sank her teeth into him, hitting the spot where she'd already claimed him before. His cock pulsed inside her again and more cum spilled out to fill her. Then he leaned heavily against her, crushing her between him and the wall as he fought for breath.

She moaned, holding tight as she felt his legs tremble, then they were both sliding to the floor in a tangle of arms and legs, his cock still buried inside her.

"Mine," she purred, licking over the wound she'd reopened.

"Yours," he answered, and she knew he was finding his way back to her.

* * * *

Logan awoke the next morning with Clara naked atop him. His back was chilled from the floor and his chest was warm from his mate. He groaned as he went to move. God, he ached all over, even his dick, which felt as if it had put in a hell of a workout. What the fuck had happened last night?

Clara stretched and blinked, her soft golden-brown eyes at him. "Logan?"

"Who else would you be naked with, Mate?" He lifted his brows with the question.

She grinned and leaned down to kiss him. "Only you." She shifted and Logan saw her try to bite off a groan.

"Are you okay?"

"Just not used to sleeping on the floor when we have a perfectly good bed upstairs."

"So why are we here on the floor?" Logan asked.

You don't remember last night?" Clara asked with huge eyes.

"I remember the alarm going off." He sat up, nearly spilling her onto the floor. "Jesus! You were shot! Are you okay? Let me see."

"I'm fine," she said and showed him her leg where there was nothing more than a scar.

But then he noticed other things, like the fingertip bruises on her hips and thighs.

"What the hell?" he demanded, trying to turn her so he could see the all of her.

She glanced down as if she didn't know what he was looking at. "These?" She indicated the bruises as if they were nothing. "Yeah, it was a great night, and they'll be gone soon."

"Fuck!" Logan exploded. "I did that to you?"

"Oh, yeah," Clara moaned. "And I enjoyed every minute of it."

"I've never bruised a woman in my life, Clara. I swear."

"I'm not only a woman. I'm your mate, and trust me. I gave as good as I got. How's your back?"

He shifted his shoulders. "Sore."

"Sorry about that," Clara crooned. "I think my claws might have come out a bit at one point."

"So I had this dream about having wild, completely no-holds-barred sex with you all night long," Logan said.

Clara shook her head. "Not a dream. Six times, stud."

"Six?" He knew his eyes had to reveal his disbelief. He had stamina, but he wasn't a machine for God's sake.

"Oh, yeah," Clara purred, looking very content. "Do you remember after I was shot?"

"I had Reno bring you back here. He's faster than me now that he's in sync with his tiger, and I knew I needed you back here as quickly as possible. I grabbed Dillion and…" His eyes widened. "The little prick jabbed me with something."

"Needle filled with feral cat fever, or at least some version of it. I think Diane may have been next door running tests most of the night."

"Shit. I hope I didn't scare her."

"I think you might have impressed her," Clara said, and Logan felt his face flush at the implication that Diane might have heard him and Clara having sex.

"So what all happened?"

"You came to me. The fever will send a shifter into a feral rage. The only thing that can calm them is their mate. You sought me out, and we made a night of it."

"And now?" Logan asked.

Clara shrugged. "I'm not really sure since I don't know exactly what strain or dosage you were given. But since you're human, it should wear off. There are no markers in your blood for it to feed on, not even with my saliva mixed in. With a shifter, it will find the very part of us that makes us shifters and feed on it, multiplying and spreading through our system."

"I'm glad it was me he got then," Logan muttered, thinking of what this could have done to Tah or Reno, Murphy or Zane. God forbid it had happened to Clara.

"It wasn't just you," Clara informed him. "Dillion only got you with some of what was in that needle."

"Who'd he get with the rest?" Logan demanded, tensing up.

"Zane."

"Where is he? Is he okay?"

"He's gone," Diane said, walking into the room to join them.

Logan pulled the sheet beside them over his lap and jerked it up to cover Clara.

"Please," Diane muttered. "I'm a doctor for God's sake. Besides, I'll be surprised if you can even get it up right now after last night's performance."

He could feel the flush under the skin starting at his pecs and rising to suffuse his entire face.

"Diane," Clara chastised and Logan had the luxury of seeing Diane blush now.

"Sorry. I guess nothing surprises me sexually when it comes to mates. But I'm getting damn tired of my lab being used as your playground."

Logan thought of when he'd first met Clara, when Reno had shifted into his tiger and come down there to find Amia. He shifted uncomfortably. "Sorry, Diane."

She waved her hand. "Anyway, I heard voices and…" She turned pleading eyes on them. "I was hoping to get some answers from you now, on what we're dealing with. What can I do to help Logan? And Zane?"

"I'm not sure," Clara said. "Why don't you give us half an hour to crawl upstairs and take a hot shower and then we'll meet everyone in the front room. I'll tell you everything I know about it then. Along with what I can about Dillion."

Diane nodded. "Are you okay? I…" She cleared her throat. "I couldn't help overhearing the two of you last night. Do you need me to check anything?"

"Jesus!" Logan muttered. "You aren't looking at my dick."

"I wasn't offering, asshole," Diane lashed back, surprising the hell out of Logan. "I just meant you were both pretty primal last night. It sounded…" She cleared her throat. "It sounded rough. I just thought I'd offer in case all the activity took a toll."

"Oh," Logan said, not sure what to say to this Diane.

"We'll be fine," Clara answered, saving him from any attempt on his part.

Diane looked at them then sighed and shrugged. "Suit yourself," she muttered and left the room as quickly as she'd entered.

"Let's head up," Clara said before he could ask her anything else.

A hot shower sounded heavenly, but he had to admit he was dreading the long trek up two flights of stairs. Not to mention the fact they were both naked. Clara rummaged in the room and came back with his jeans and shirt. She pulled his shirt on and tossed him the jeans. Then she reached down and grabbed his socks, shoes and boxer briefs from the floor then turned back to him.

"Ready?" she asked.

He nodded, and they made their way carefully up the stairs. Either the fates were with them or Diane had called up to warn everyone to give them some privacy, because they didn't run into anyone on the main floor or on the way up to their second-floor bedroom. Clara tossed his stuff on the floor inside the door and stripped his shirt off before he even had the door completely shut.

"God, I need a shower," she exclaimed, and he got his first look at her back.

"Shit," he thundered, walking over to her and taking in the tiny bruises marring her perfect flesh. "What did I do to you? And why are these not healing? Does it hurt?"

"Everything I wanted and more," she said. "That's what you did. I'm sure they have healed a bit. They're pretty light, Logan."

His face must have shown how much that comment hit him because she cupped his face and held his gaze.

"I swear. You didn't hurt me."

She grabbed his hand and tugged him into the bathroom, turning him to face the mirror. He'd been so focused on her then Diane walking in on them and discussing things, that he hadn't once taken stock of himself. He'd noticed some scratches but not thought much of them. Now he realized there were a lot of them. He also had some bruises of his own.

"Damn woman! What did you do to me?"

"Everything you wanted me to," she said with that sexy purr of hers.

"Not a dream, huh," he said, shaking his head and reliving every moment he thought he'd only dreamed. "Standing up?"

"Hell, yeah," Clara groaned. "You were fucking amazing."

"Guess that explains why my thighs are sore."

She laughed. "Mine, too."

She leaned in the shower and started the water while he grabbed towels. She was already sighing beneath the spray when he placed them on the towel bar.

"Are you sure I didn't hurt you?" he asked again when he joined her.

"Logan," she whispered, leaning back into his chest. "You're my mate. The only way you hurt me is if you leave me."

"Never," he swore. "I know this has all been really fast, and there's so much we still don't know about one another. But I'm looking forward to spending the rest of my life learning all of those things."

She turned in his arms and snuggled close while the water washed over them both. "Me, too," she whispered. "Me, too."

Chapter Fifteen

Everyone was assembled and waiting for them when Clara walked in with Logan. Her thoughts raced in her head, and she said a little prayer for her Uncle Thomas as well as Gideon, Ariel and Griffin. God, what if… She couldn't even complete the thought.

"Good to see you both," Tah said by way of greeting. "Have to admit, I was a little worried last night when we left you."

Logan looked a little embarrassed, so Clara spoke up. "We're great. Logan seems to be back to himself this morning. Do you have any results yet, Diane, on what he was given?"

"A lower grade form of the feral cat fever virus," the Professor answered. "I spent most of the night researching, pulling information from every source I could think of. What this looks like is that somebody took a full-strength strain of this virus and has been watering it down. It will cause similar effects in shifters, though obviously at a higher level. There's no record of it being used on humans that I can find."

"And Dillion is the one who had it?" Clara asked.

"Yes," Reno snapped. "I saw the bastard shoot what he didn't get into Logan into Zane."

"But you didn't see the needle before he put it in Zane?" Clara wanted to know.

Reno shook his head.

"Why does it matter?" Abby asked.

"Because that means we don't know how much Zane got and how much Logan got," Diane answered.

Clara nodded in agreement. "Exactly."

"So we go beat it out of the little shit who knocked me out and make the rat bastard tell us," Vic grumbled from the couch.

"How did he get to you?" Logan asked.

The other woman compressed her lips in a tight line of disgust. "I ran into Lydia and had my attention on her. I didn't even hear him come up behind me. Then boom. Lights out. Next thing I know I'm waking up with Amia leaning over me."

"When I found you guys, Amia and Lydia were yelling at each other," Clara said.

Amia snorted. "Good old Lydia wanted to shoot me, to rid the world of Marcus's foul spawn."

"That woman is batshit crazy," Reno said.

"Are they both still in the storage rooms you said you were taking them to?" Clara asked.

"For now," Tah nodded. "We don't have any other place to put them at the moment."

"What about the room I was in?" Clara asked.

"I won't have her on the same floor as my mate," Reno said with a deep growl.

Clara nodded. "Understood." She blew out a heavy sigh. "Let me start with telling you guys a little about Dillion. If there's anyone more hell-bent on revenge than Lydia, it's him."

"Why?" Abby asked.

"His entire family was wiped out by hunters. He was the only one hidden when they got there. But he heard everything while his parents and two sisters were tortured and murdered. My uncle found him a short time after. We don't know how long he was on his own."

"Jesus," Tah muttered, squeezing the bridge of his nose. "The more I hear of these hunters, the more I question if the answer isn't to just go in and kill them all."

"At what cost?" Clara asked, then waved her hand, not willing to get sidetracked on that discussion again. "Let me finish. Dillion has been obsessed with revenge since I've known him. He stayed with a family of shifters near us after the murders. He's always in and out of my Uncle Thomas's shop. Dillion's three years younger than me."

"So how did Dillion get his hands on a vial of this stuff?" Diana demanded, and Clara understood the other woman's need for answers.

"My uncle travels a lot. He finds not just people but things. He's been attacked several times by hunters. One group of them gave him a dosage of the fever," Clara answered.

"What happened to him?" Diane asked. "And how the hell did he manage not to get killed?"

"He doesn't really talk about it. Except for when he was given the drug. I was just a toddler at the time, but I can tell you what I've heard. He tore himself off the wall and killed every single one of them in the room with him. The hunters didn't realize what it would do to a shifter. He was able to find his way back to us and brought a pretty good supply of it with him. He planned to study it."

"How did he fight the effects of the virus?" Diane demanded.

"He was mated," Clara answered.

"How does that make a difference?" Abby wanted to know.

"Mated shifters are linked to another person. That means in times of great crisis, we look to them as our strength. We connect at a primal level. Soul-to-soul. So when we are stripped back down to that primal level, we look for that which soothes us. Our mates. It's instinct to find our mate," Clara said and noticed the way Diane paled a little. "Mates are the only ones to calm us in those moments. They are also the only ones safe. A shifter will never harm his or her mate. Never."

"I know that," Abby said, smiling at Tah.

"So what about Zane?" Reno questioned.

"Not knowing how much he was hit with..." Clara said with a shrug. "All we can do is wait and see. If he had a mate, it would be a different story. She would be able to find him and bring him back. But without her..." She shrugged again.

"So are you thinking Dillion got a hold of some of those vials?" Logan asked.

Clara nodded. "That's all I can figure. I know Uncle Thomas has questioned over the years if he was missing some. A vial here or there, never enough to make him think someone was deliberately stealing it, or at least not that I remember. And now. God, now I don't know what's going on."

"Do you think this could have something to do with why your uncle is gone?" Vic asked.

"It could. I knew something was wrong. My uncle doesn't normally stay gone for longer than a week at a time. Then Lydia said Gideon left to search for him, taking Griffin and Ariel with him. Gideon grew up with my dad and uncle. He's..." She searched for a way to describe him. "He's a different cup of tea."

"What do you mean?" Amia asked.

"He's a loner. Most of us tend to be social. Gideon doesn't like groups. He prefers to keep to himself," Clara said.

"Sounds like a guy after my own heart," Vic muttered.

"So you don't think he'd go searching for your uncle?" Tah asked.

"No, he would," Clara confirmed. "But he'd go on his own. I could see him maybe taking Griffin with him if he absolutely had to, but he'd never take a woman with him."

"Why the fuck not?" Vic demanded.

"Because he feels women are to be protected at all costs," Clara said.

"That's not such a bad trait in a man," Abby said. "Tah does that."

"You think Dillion and Lydia might have done something to them?" the Professor asked.

Clara nodded. "My uncle's mate is dead. The other three are all unmated. If he shot them with this stuff." She shook her head, and Logan stepped over and wrapped his arms around her, pulling her against his chest and rubbing his hands up and down her arms to comfort her.

"We got a problem," Finn said as he entered the room. "Two of them actually."

Clara felt extremely bad that she hadn't even noticed that Finn and Murphy hadn't been in the room.

"What is it?" Tah asked.

"That little asshole is driving me fucking crazy," Finn stated bluntly. "He's shifted and is ramming into the door. He's either going to knock himself out or I'm going to open the fucking door and knock him out."

"Let him beat his head on the door!" Diane exclaimed, bringing all eyes to her. "After what he's done, he can rot for all I care," she said.

"As good as that sounds, we do need answers from him," Clara said, breaking the stunned silence. Diane was not one to normally make blood-thirsty statements. "We might not want him to hurt himself too badly before we get them."

"Fuck," Tah said. "What did he shift into?"

"Looks like a cougar," Finn said. "Nothing I can't knock the fuck out."

"Was there any of what Lydia used left in the bullet you pulled out, Diane?" Tah asked.

"Already on it," Diane said.

"I've been analyzing it, trying to see what exactly it is," the Professor said and rubbed his eyes. "I could really use some more eyes down in the lab. The amount of work we're doing is much more than two people should try to handle."

"I'll help out any way I can," Abby said.

"Not right now," Tah countered, earning a glare from his mate.

"He's right," the Professor intervened. "You need to concentrate on the baby right now."

"There's one more thing," Finn said.

"Shit!" Reno said. "What else?"

"It's the woman. Lydia?"

"What about her?" Clara asked, tensing up. No matter how hard she tried, she could never forget the woman who had walked in the first day. That had been a woman devastated by leaving her daughter behind, and one willing to take on a fatherless shifter. Clara would have sworn Lydia was starting to heal when suddenly she started growing angrier and angrier.

"She's not looking so good. I'd swear she's going through some type of withdrawal," Finn said.

"Oh, my God," Clara said as things clicked together in her mind. "What if Dillion's been drugging her all along? For years? Right under our noses?"

"Dillion?" Amia asked. "You think he's been drugging my mom?"

"Her sudden surge back to anger, her need to kill all hunters, all Blanes, even you," Clara said. "It all started right around the time Dillion arrived. Jesus! Why didn't I ever notice that? Why didn't my uncle or Gideon? She and Dillion aren't in the same room are they?"

Logan shook his head. "Those rooms are too tiny to even hold one person, much less two."

"If he's been giving her doses of the virus to feed her anger… Over that extended period of time… We're talking years here," the Professor mused. "She might never recover from it." He stood up and pointed to Finn. "You come with me. I'll need blood samples from her. Diane, check and see if we have anything on hand that might help with detoxification."

"I'll help," Vic said and crossed the room to go with them. She stopped in front of Clara. "For what it's worth, I'm sorry for my part in what happened with you. I saw an opportunity, and I took it. My mistake. I take full responsibility for it. I'll understand if you want me to leave."

"I don't have the right to ask anyone to leave," Clara said, a little shocked.

"You're a mate," Vic stated. "You have every right."

Clara shook her head. "I still wouldn't. In your place, I'd have done the same thing."

Vic smiled and shook her head. "No, you wouldn't have. You're too kind-hearted for that. Abby told me what you said. You want to believe we don't need to become the beast. I say fuck it and embrace the beast. I fight to win."

"The end justifies the means," Clara quoted.

"I always did love Machiavelli," Vic said.

"I like you," Clara quipped.

"You're all right, too," Vic agreed.

Clara took the hand Vic held out. The woman had a firm handshake. Then Vic turned and left the room without another word.

"I'm glad that's settled," Abby said. "I know it was bothering Vic."

"How could you tell?" Clara asked.

Abby laughed. "She may seem hardnosed, but you'll figure her out the more you get to know her."

"I'm honestly going to look forward to that," Clara stated.

"Logan, I'm going to want you in the lab giving blood as often as the Professor requests. Until we know for sure that this feral fever is out of your system, I want you to stick close to the house," Tah interjected.

"We can't afford for you to pull me off rotation," Logan argued.

"We can't afford to have you out there if that stuff is still churning away inside you. You could hurt someone. I know you don't want that," Tah told him.

"You're right," Logan admitted.

"I can stick with him," Clara offered. "We were supposed to be put on rotation together anyway. It would make even more sense to keep us together now. If anything happens while I'm with him, I'll call one of you to cover for us and head back to the cabin with Logan."

Tah looked up and rocked his head back and forth for a moment before nodding. "That makes sense. We do need everyone we have."

"That reminds me," Logan said. "Clara had a really good idea."

"Oh, yeah?" Tah asked, glancing at her.

"I just mentioned to Logan that you take a lot of the responsibility for things on yourself," she said.

"I'm the head of the pride," Tah said. There was no arrogance in his statement, just a declaration of fact.

"You are," she agreed. "And as such, your primary focus should be on the protection of the pride. You could set up a council of sorts, a group that you trust to oversee the other areas. That way you're not pulled in a million directions. Plus, it gives others in the pride a sense of value. Shifters have been doing it for years."

"Why didn't I think of that?" Abby mused. "It's a brilliant idea."

Tah looked fixedly at Clara, to the point she wanted to squirm. Then he blew her away by walking over and hugging her to him. "It is a brilliant idea. Thank you. And welcome to the pride, little sister."

Clara blinked rapidly, not wanting to cry in front of everyone. But they had no clue what it meant to her to be embraced and welcomed by Tah, to have him call her little sister.

"I think she's a little choked up," Logan said.

"Thank you," she finally managed.

"We'll do our best to find some way of searching for your uncle and friends," Tah promised. "I don't know when, but we'll do our best."

"I understand," Clara said, and she did.

Zane was gone. Finn was still without a memory of where he'd been and what had happened. Lydia might have been getting slowly poisoned over the last few years and regardless, she was focused on killing Amia at the moment. And Logan might or might not have more of the virus in him. There was so much going on here. She would have to accept that it could be a while before she could go in search of her uncle or the others.

There was knock on the front door and they all jumped. Who the hell was knocking on the door?

"Stay here," Tah ordered Abby. "You two keep an eye on her." He pointed to Amia and Clara then he, Logan and Reno stepped into the hall in front of the door.

"Who are you and how the hell did you get here?" Tah demanded of whoever was there.

"Walked right in," a familiar voice said. "Did you expect your alarms to keep shifters out?"

Clara turned and walked out in the hall, a grin wide on her face. "Orsai!" she called.

"Well, hello there, baby girl. It's good to see you again. Thomas here?"

She shook her head as she went to step forward, but Logan grabbed her and Tah and Reno both stepped in front of her.

"What are you doing here?" Tah asked.

"I heard my nephew was here," Orsai said. "I came to find him."

"Orsai?" Reno said. "This is the guy you said taught you everything. The one we couldn't find, we'd have to wait for him to find us?"

"Consider yourself found," Orsai said with a sparkling white smile bright against the ebony of his skin.

"Who's your nephew?" Tah asked, but Clara knew they'd already figured it out.

"Zane," she answered anyway, and Orsai nodded in agreement.

"I've traveled a long way to see him," Orsai said.

"Come on in," Tah finally said and held the door wide. "We've got a lot to tell you, and we could use your help."

"Always glad to help," Orsai said. "Especially the Tah." He bowed low before Tah.

"I'm so glad you're here," Clara told him as he walked past her and patted her on the shoulder.

"There will be more, and soon, "Orsai said. "I can feel the winds of change. Soon," he murmured. "Soon."

Chapter Sixteen

Orsai had agreed to stay on indefinitely until they found Zane. He didn't seem overly concerned about his nephew having gotten injected with the feral fever virus. Orsai seemed to believe Zane's mate would find him, and he would be better and happier than he'd ever been.

He was also smitten with Abby and declared he would be around to see her first child into the world. He said he'd seen that she would need him and that was that. Diane seemed both relieved and anxious to have him around. The Professor loved it. The two men got along like old friends and spent most evenings together chatting. Orsai truly was a fountain of wisdom and had jumped right in to help in the labs. He was fascinated by all that the Professor and Diane had managed to do alone.

Tonight was the night they finally got to have the celebration Logan had planned. Tables were overflowing with food and for the first time, Clara saw them drinking beer. Orsai declared there'd be no trouble tonight and Tah, in a show of faith, hadn't put anyone out on patrol, allowing everyone to stay in and celebrate. Clara noticed they were nursing the beers, all of them. Apparently a show of faith didn't mean they wouldn't be prepared.

"There you are," Logan said, coming up behind her and wrapping his arms around her.

"I'm never far from you," she promised

"Come with me," he urged. "I have something to ask of you."

"Anything," Clara assured him.

He took her hand, and she followed him into the house.

"I need you to help keep Abby busy for a bit, while we set some things up," Logan said. "Amia is going to help you. I can't tell you what's going on. But I promise you it's fantastic. Something we all need, but especially Tah and Abby."

"Okay," Clara agreed. "How long do you need us to keep her?"

"Only half an hour," Logan promised. "The Professor will come get you guys when things are ready."

Clara grinned. "Is this one of those dreams-coming-true moments for women?"

"I hope so," Logan said. "And with Orsai here, it's going to be even better."

Logan bent to kiss her and reached around to pat her ass. "If I haven't told you yet, you look absolutely stunning in that dress. I'm having trouble tearing my eyes away from you."

"You've told me at least a dozen times," Clara said with a laugh.

"And I'll tell you at least that many more," he vowed. "I'm so lucky you found me."

She nodded in agreement. He gave her another kiss and reluctantly turned to leave her. Clara went in search of Abby and Amia and found them both in Abby's room with the door open.

"Thank God, you're here, Clara," Amia said. "Abby's lost her ring and she's getting a little frantic to find it."

"What ring?" Clara asked, walking in to join them.

"Tah gave it to me after he asked me to marry him," Abby said. "I took it off when I was having all the issues with the pregnancy. My fingers were so swollen. Now that they're back to a more normal size, I thought I'd put it back on. But I can't find it."

"Well, let's take a break and sit down for a minute. I could use some girl talk, and you two look like you could use a short break to relax and get your bearings. The harder you look for something, the harder it usually is to find it."

"You're right," Abby agreed, rubbing her belly and going over to sit on the bed. She eased back against the pillow and sighed. "Join me," she said and patted the bed.

"Thirteen weeks now," Clara commented. "That little lion is going to be here before you know it. Two weeks. Maybe three."

"I think he'll be here in less than two weeks, maybe ten days from now," Abby said. "I just feel it. It's like he's letting me know he's ready to be here."

"Then we'll make sure everything's ready," Amia said. "First thing is to get that crib put together over there."

Abby sighed. "With all we've had going on, there just hasn't been time. I still need to get some of the clothes washed and ready to go, set up the changing table, and Tah wants one of the playpens set up in the office as well as the lab. And then there's the childproofing. I have no idea how to childproof, much less for a shifter."

Clara laughed. "Good luck with that. Cats are curious by nature and into everything. Besides, you have time. He won't be crawling for a while. And you have all of us to help you."

"What's it like?" Amia spoke up.

"Being pregnant?" Abby asked and Amia nodded. "It's the most wonderful thing in the world. To hold this tiny life inside you and know that he's not just a part of me but a part of his father as well, a living, breathing symbol of the love Tah and I share. To watch my big, strong mate go to his knees and croon to my belly, shower it with kisses and promises." She shook her head. "There are no words to express how it feels."

"And even before, when you could feel yourself getting weaker?" Amia asked.

"Even then, I was happy," Abby said. "I'm guessing pregnancy is different for every woman. For me, it's been the second greatest blessing of my life. The first being Tah. Not even second really, but more like an addition to the first. I can't wait to hold my little guy in my arms."

"What's up, Amia?" Clara asked.

Amia blew out a deep breath. "I think I might be getting ready to ovulate. My ovaries were cramping a bit this morning. I don't have a normal cycle like some women, but my ovaries usually let me know when they're getting ready to work."

"And you're worried?" Abby asked.

“I’m not sure I’m ready to be a mother,” Amia admitted. “And watching you. It’s been a little terrifying.”

Abby nodded. “We know more now though. Thanks to Clara.”

“Besides,” Clara added. “Ovulation and heat don’t guarantee a pregnancy. It could be years before you and Reno have kids. When it’s meant, it will happen.”

“What about you, Clara?” Amia asked. “Do you want kids?”

Clara thought about holding a baby in her arms, a son who looked like Logan. “Someday,” she admitted. “Whenever Logan and I are blessed with one. I have no control over it. And neither do you, Amia. Unfortunately, that’s the way of shifters. Human forms of birth control don’t work for us. Not pills, shots, implants or condoms. Nature gets what nature wants.”

Abby reached for Amia’s hand then Clara’s. “I’m so glad the two of you are here. That Reno and Logan were both blessed with two such remarkable women. I don’t think it was chance, the way you two are connected. Despite the reasons why, you essentially shared a mother, making you more like sisters than you realize. And Logan and Reno are more than friends. Even when they weren’t with Tah, they were with each other. The four of you… It warms my heart to see you getting along now.”

“I didn’t know Reno and Logan grew up together,” Clara said.

“They didn’t,” Abby replied. “But once they met each other in the Marines, they stuck. When they all left it behind and went their separate ways, Logan and Reno remained together.”

“Oh,” Clara said.

“I knew they were close,” Amia admitted. “Reno speaks of Tah and Logan all the time. He loves them.”

“They all love each other, and we love them,” Abby said. “Sometimes family isn’t the group of people you’re born into. Sometimes it’s the people you chose. Those three chose each other, and then they chose us. It’s up to us to choose them back and band together for them. We are the core of this pride we’re building, the foundation. They are the walls, but walls can’t stand if the foundation is shaky. We have to be rocks, ladies. For them and for each other.”

Clara felt her eyes get a little misty and blinked several times. It was easy to see it wasn't just Tah that Abby loved. She took them all to her heart, everyone around her. Clara had seen her extremely fierce and had felt the bite of Abby's anger herself. She'd also been embraced by the warmth of Abby's love and acceptance. She was exactly the woman the Tah would need by his side, the woman they would all need.

There was a knock at the door before either Clara or Amia could say anything back.

"Come in," Abby called and the Professor poked his head around.

"I thought I'd see if I could come escort the prettiest woman in the world to the festivities tonight. I think your absence is being noticed, my dear," the Professor told Abby.

"We should go, too," Amia said, sharing a look with Clara. "We'll see you out there."

"I'll be right there," Abby said.

Clara and Amia hurried out of the room.

"Did Reno tell you what was going on?" Clara asked.

"No, but I have my suspicions." Amia stopped and turned to face Clara. "Abby's right you know. We are sisters. I'm so sorry for the things I've said, for hitting you simply because I couldn't deal with my own shit. Can you really forgive me?"

"I hear siblings fight a lot," Clara said. "Can you ever forgive me for not going in after you?"

"You did what you could," Amia said. "Doing anything more could have gotten you killed."

"I just—"

"No," Amia interrupted. "We start fresh, here and now. Leave the past in the past and only move forward."

Clara nodded. "I…I need to tell you something first. I can't hate her, Amia. No matter how much I try to only hear the mean and foul words Lydia has said over the last several years, I still see the woman who woke up crying and calling your name."

"I'm trying," Amia admitted. "Thinking she was dead. Knowing she isn't. Dealing with the possibility she's been drugged. It's a lot to take in, but I'm trying. I really am."

"I'm here for you," Clara promised. "Any questions or even if you just want to talk. I'm here."

Amia smiled. "Thank you. Same goes."

Clara squeezed Amia's hand. "Let's go find our mates."

"Sounds like a plan," Amia agreed.

Clara's breath caught as they stepped out on the porch. It had been transformed by strings of lights and candles. Flowers were everywhere and there was now an aisle of sorts leading up to a beautiful arch wrapped in vines and flowers. Tah and Orsai stood in front of it. Reno stepped forward and whispered something to Amia, then took her arm and led her down the aisle where they separated. He stood by Tah, while she stood on the other side.

Logan stepped up to Clara.

"Would you do me the honor of walking with me?" he whispered.

"Are they getting married?" she whispered back.

"It's past time," Logan answered with a nod. "We've let too much force us to push the important things to the back burner. So tonight, we celebrate, and what better to celebrate than love?"

She nodded and sniffled a little. It was beautiful, and she was so happy for Abby and Tah. Logan held his arm out to her and she took it, matching her stride to his as they walked down the aisle. Before they separated he took her hand and kissed her palm, then walked to stand beside Reno and Tah while she stepped over beside Amia.

Abby appeared with the Professor and Clara could see the joy on the other woman's face. It lit up the night better than any candle or light could. Her gaze seemed to find Tah's and lock there. She didn't tremble, didn't falter. She walked straight to her mate and took his hand.

"This explains the ring," Amia whispered to Clara, and they shared a grin.

The ceremony was beautiful. Clara hadn't known Orsai could perform weddings, but then nothing about him really surprised her. And did it matter? What was a piece of paper to them? A shifter mated for life. There was no fear of falling out of love or divorce or any of the issues their human counterparts faced. There was actually a beautiful ceremony that the shifters observed, as well. She'd have to talk to Logan about it.

Applause and shouts filled the air around them as Tah kissed his bride.

"Now I ask that all three mated couples step forward," Orsai said once things had quieted down a bit.

Logan walked over to stand with her, and Reno held his hand out for Amia to join him on the other side of Tah and Abby.

"What's going on?" Clara whispered, but Logan just smiled.

"A shifter is never fully alive until he or she finds their other half. For us, there is only ever one person who will complete us. Some never find that person. Some find them, only to lose them too soon. But when we do find our one true mate, it is important to give thanks and pledge before the Great Creator and all those we claim as family, that our bond is true and lasting." Orsai looked at all three couples, and Clara felt warmed by his smile when he glanced at her and Logan. "So tonight we not only celebrate the ritual of marriage as ordained by the laws of man, but the ritual of life mates as ordained by the Great Creator."

He turned to Reno and Amia on the end. "Reno and Amia, do you admit you are mates? Joined in hearts, bound by spirit?"

Amia and Reno shared a look, and Clara saw tears in Amia's eyes.

"We do," they answered together.

"Tah and Abby, do you admit you are mates? Joined in hearts, bound by spirit?"

"We do." Their voices were strong and loud as they looked at each other with love.

Clara held her breath as Orsai turned to her and Logan.

"Logan and Clara, do you admit you are mates? Joined in heart, bound by spirit?"

Clara nodded, blinking her own tears as Logan smiled at her.

"We do," they answered.

"Now I will ask the men to repeat after me." Orsai lifted his hands toward the sky. "In the name of the Great Creator who has blessed us, by the life that flows within my veins and the love that flows within my heart, I take you as mine for now and always."

Clara felt her tears splashing over as Logan's strong voice repeated the words. He looked only at her, and she could see he meant every word he was saying.

"To my heart, of my spirit, as my life's mate unto death and beyond. I shall possess you and be possessed by you, so that none may come between us. I am yours."

Logan squeezed her hand as he finished the vows, and she thought his eyes might be a little misty, too.

"Now I will have the three ladies repeat after me," Orsai said. "In the name of the Great Creator who has blessed us, by the life that flows within my veins and the love that flows within my heart, I take you as mine for now and always."

Clara's voice cracked a bit from the deep emotions going through her. She hoped her face showed Logan how much she meant the words she was repeating.

"To my heart, of my spirit, as my life's mate unto death and beyond. I shall cleave to you and be cleaved by you, so that none may come between us. I am yours."

Clara whispered the last words, so choked with emotion. So many times she'd pictured this, meeting her mate and saying these words. But this, standing here with Logan and the two other couples, was more perfect than words could convey. And she heard Abby's words in her head again.

Those three chose each other, and then they chose us. It's up to us to choose them back and band together for them.

Had Abby somehow known what Tah, Reno and Logan had planned? It wouldn't surprise Clara one bit if Abby had.

"In the name of the Great Creator, I proclaim you mates. One heart. One soul. One life."

Clara wasn't prepared for the way they handled the next part. Logan turned and took Abby's hand. She smiled at him then at Clara. Tah took Amia's hand and Logan urged Clara to move in until she and Reno could join hands as well. They stood in a circle, completely joined when they repeated the words.

"One heart. One soul. One life."

Logan looked at her. "I love you," he said loud and clear.

"I love you," she answered back, and felt a fresh wave of tears spill over.

He grinned as they dropped hands and he moved in, sweeping her off her feet and swinging her around. "Are you ready to celebrate?"

"Absolutely," she said, cupping his face.

"Good. I have one more surprise for you." He led her over to the porch steps and pointed toward one of the gliders. "Have a seat."

He turned around and grabbed something that had been leaning against the porch. The guitar she'd picked up for him. He pulled the strap over his head and adjusted it until he was satisfied. He strummed a few notes then began playing. It was just one more thing her mate was perfect at. She knew she had a goofy smile, but she didn't care. She'd never been so happy.

Soon everyone was walking over to join them. People were just plopping down to sit wherever they could find a spot. Then Finn asked if Logan could still play the ones they used to sing together. Next thing she knew, not only was Logan playing but they were all singing along. Abby was laughing, looking as if she might burst with it as she sat on the porch swing with Tah.

Finn and Murphy were singing at the top of their lungs. Tah and Reno were joining in as well as Holt. Vic was shaking her head but smiling while Kenzie quietly watched. Orsai and the Professor had disappeared inside, no doubt heading down to check on the two prisoners. Everyone had taken a turn away from the festivities at one point to check on Lydia and Dillion.

Clara soaked it all in. The comradeship they all shared. It was different from what she was used to seeing between her Uncle Thomas and Gideon. She knew the two men cared for each other, but they weren't very demonstrative about it. Here, everyone was affectionate, and Clara felt free to be the same. Diane brushed by her and touched Clara's shoulder. Clara saw sadness behind the smile on Diane's lips. It felt natural to reach up and grab the other woman's hand, tugging her down to sit beside Clara.

"Everything's going to be okay," Clara told her.

Clara felt Logan's gaze on her again and glanced over to meet it. Such love shown on his face, love she'd been afraid to even hope for.

"There's one thing you can count on in this crazy world we exist in," she told Diane.

"What's that?"

"No matter what the obstacle, love will always find away."

About the Author

Lacey Thorn spends her days in small town Indiana, the proud mother of three. When she is not busy with one of them, she can be found typing away on her computer keyboard or burying her nose in a good book. Like every woman, she knows just how chaotic life can be and how appealing that great escape can look.

So, toss aside the stress and tension of the never-ending to-do list. For now sit back, relax, and enjoy the ride with Lacey. It's your world...unlaced.

Lacey loves to talk to her readers and can be found at www.lacythorn.com. Join Lacey on Facebook at: http://www.facebook.com/#!/authorlaceythorn Or on Twitter at @laceythorn1 And feel free to email the author at lcy_thrn1@yahoo.com.

Also Available from
Resplendence Publishing

Serephin **by Lacey Thorn**

Demon Chronicles Series, Book One

Serephin wanted to be loved. But being half human and half demon made her an outcast. So, together with her two best friends, she heads to the human world hoping that since they look human, they will find a home there. But nothing is as they read. They are no longer outcasts, but if their demon blood is discovered they will become the hunted.

Morgin and Drallan vow to protect Serephin as long as she agrees to become their mate. Serephin can't admit what she is and her mates have secrets of their own. Can the threesome find a way to trust and form a bond that includes love?

Swallowing His Pride **by Serena Pettus**

Southern Pride Series, Book One

Welcome to Pride, Texas, the home of cowboys, roughnecks, southern charm…and shifters. Lion shifters to be exact.

When a trip to Las Vegas has Dylan coming face to face with a woman who calls to every part of him—especially his inner lion—he's not sure what to do. Yearning to spend as much time with her as possible, Dylan courts her until one night of passion takes things further than even he was prepared to go. She's now his mate.

The impromptu vacation Samantha took with her best friend took a turn for the better when a hunky guy with a charming southern accent takes a liking to her. Unable to deny the intense chemistry between them, she tosses her inhibitions to the wind and indulges in a night of carnal bliss…only to wake up alone.

Hurt and confused, she heads home, only to discover that not everything that happens in Vegas stays there. Now he's back, and she must decide what to do once he confesses a secret that turns her reality on its head. But now there's a danger lurking in the shadows as well. A threat that is determined to keep humans out of the shifter society…by any means necessary.

Dragon's Blood **by Brynn Paulin**

Cruentus Dragons Series, Book One

For centuries, there have been legends of Vampires—the fault of one careless dragon. But humans only know part of the story. Walking amongst us are Dragons—Shape-shifters who feed on blood.

Reluctant Dragon Elder Janos Aventech's vacation in New York is about to come to an abrupt end. Riding on the subway, he stumbles across a Dragon mate—one of the few human women with whom his people can unite and be truly happy. And his people's enemies are out to get her. As his attraction to this woman grows, he knows he must find her mate and see her safely into that man's arms. It's destined. But as every minute passes in her company, Janos begins to see he'll never willingly let her go, mate or not.

If only she were his mate…

On the subway, Scarlett couldn't stop staring at him—then he turned crazy. When he essentially kidnaps her off the train, she knows she should be irate and terrified. Instead, she finds her initial attraction growing. But what's all this stuff he's spouting about mates and enemies? She only wants to return to her life, not get caught in the middle of a war. But it's too late for that. She's destined for a Dragon's bed, and in Janos' arms, she can only hope it's his.

Eternal Flame **by Valerie Twombly**

Guardians Series, Book One

A woman he cannot have, a man who is only a dream...

When guardian Marcus Dagotto, discovers the gods have gifted him with a mate, he is pissed. He has no room for love and even less for a human who has no idea he exists.

Cassandra Jensen, has a shattered heart and has given up on men. Only one man can set her body on fire, but he is a fantasy that haunts her sleep.

Two worlds, one desire. When the two collide, fate will rip them apart and test their resolve. Will darkness and evil prevail? Or, will love conquer all?

Rules of Darkness **by Tia Fanning**

One special gift...Twelve rules to follow...There are some rules that should never be broken.

They tell me that I am special, that my ability to heal is a "gift" that should be treasured and appreciated. As far as I'm concerned, I'm not gifted...I'm cursed. Nothing in this life is free, not even gifts. There is always a price to be paid somewhere, somehow.

My healing gift came with twelve Rules of Darkness, rules that I must follow at all times, until the day I die. The rules are ingrained in who I am. They dictate how I live my life when I am awake, and they haunt me when I'm asleep. Don't look into a graveyard, Katia.

Don't touch the dead, Katia. Never seek out the lost, Katia...It's enough to drive a person mad.

And perhaps that's where I find myself now. A victim of a disease I can cure in others, but not in myself. It's madness to break the rules, and yet, I don't care anymore. I'm tired of living my life this way. I'm tired of the rules. I won't do it anymore, and if that means I suffer the consequences, then so be it.

www.resplendencepublishing.com

26244186R00104

Made in the USA
San Bernardino, CA
22 November 2015